ALSO BY
ROBIN LIPPINCOTT

The Real, True Angel

Mr.
Dalloway

—— A NOVELLA ——

Robin Lippincott

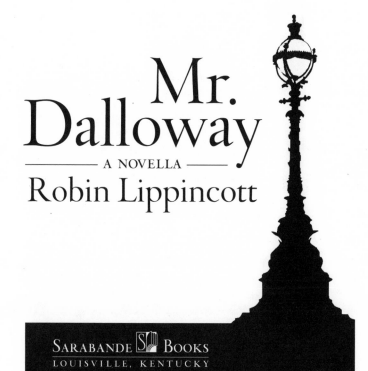

SARABANDE BOOKS
LOUISVILLE, KENTUCKY

Managing Editor
Sarabande Books, Inc.
2234 Dundee Road, Suite 200
Louisville, KY 40205

LIBRARY OF CONGRESS CATALOGING-IN-PUBLICATION DATA

Lippincott, Robin.
Mr. Dalloway : a novella / Robin Lippincott.
p.   cm.
ISBN 1-889330-28-0 (cloth : alk. paper). – ISBN 1-889330-29-9 (pbk. : alk. paper)
I. Title.
PS3562.I583M7   1999
813'.54–dc21   98-31006
CIP

Cover photograph: Horace A. Murch, *Westminster Nightfall*. Used by permission
of The Royal Photographic Society, Bath, England.

Cover and text design by Charles Casey Martin.

Manufactured in the United States of America.
This book is printed on acid-free paper.

Sarabande Books is a nonprofit literary organization.

To
Sena Jeter Naslund

·

But, looking for a phrase,
I found none to stand
beside your name

"Literary character is always an invention, and inventions generally are indebted to prior inventions."

HAROLD BLOOM
"The Analysis of Character"
Major Literary Characters: Clarissa Dalloway

Extracts

—"No one understood until I met Richard. He gave me all I wanted. He's man and woman." Clarissa Dalloway, *The Voyage Out,* Virginia Woolf.

—"I didn't get on well with my father." Richard Dalloway, *The Voyage Out,* Virginia Woolf.

—"For in marriage a little license, a little independence there must be between people living together day in day out in the same house; which Richard gave her, and she him. (Where was he this morning for instance? Some committee, she never asked what)." Clarissa Dalloway, *Mrs. Dalloway,* Virginia Woolf.

—"Mr. Dalloway, ma'am, told me to tell you he would be lunching out." Lucy the maid, *Mrs. Dalloway,* Virginia Woolf.

—"Richard always kept himself in the pink of condition." Lady Bruton on Mr. Dalloway, *Mrs. Dalloway,* Virginia Woolf.

—"…the soul…is by nature unmated, a widow bird…." Sasha Latham, "A Summing Up," *Mrs. Dalloway's Party,* Virginia Woolf.

—"And there is a dignity in people; a solitude; even between husband and wife a gulf; and that one must respect, thought Clarissa Dalloway…for one would not part with oneself, or take it, against his will, from one's husband, without losing one's independence, one's self-respect—something, after all, priceless." *Mrs. Dalloway,* Virginia Woolf.

—"The ship lurched. Rachel fell slightly forward. Richard took her in his arms and kissed her…. 'You tempt me,' he said. The tone of his voice was terrifying. He seemed choked in fight." *The Voyage Out,* Virginia Woolf.

—"No vulgar jealousy could separate her from Richard." Clarissa Dalloway, *Mrs. Dalloway,* Virginia Woolf.

—"By the way, I meant Richard Dalloway to be liked." Virginia Woolf to Philip Morrell, 27 July 1925, *The Letters of Virginia Woolf, Volume Three.*

CONTENTS

PART ONE
28 June, 1927

Mr. Dalloway said he would buy the flowers himself.

For he wanted to surround Clarissa with them; to choose those flowers, those colours, which would set her off to the best possible advantage; which would complement her. But what colours those would be, he had no idea. And so he had asked Lucy (now he was applying his bowler hat as he examined himself in the hallway looking-glass). And what was it Lucy had said (she was polishing silver at the time; he remembered the refracted artificial light slicing through the room): pinks; lavenders; shades of yellow; periwinkle blues? "Pale colours, sir," he thought she had said. Yes (he straightened his tie), that was it.

Clarissa deserved it after all. For she (he thought now, pausing in the hallway and broodily pondering the past year, as a dark cloud may race across the sky on an otherwise sunny day), she has been entirely patient and good throughout all of this. It was a phrase which had first come to him months ago, one which now, upon occasion, repeated itself—a banner marched to and fro across the floor of his brain: *Clarissa has been entirely patient and good throughout all of this* (he might have declared on the floor of the House). Perhaps it was because she had surprised him so much, by her response: her tolerance, her goodness, her acceptance (and *because* of his lack of those qualities? he wondered now). And because it was true (the truth does resound, he thought). He picked up his umbrella.

"I understand," she had said.

And so he was off (Big Ben chimed the hour—ten o'clock); out the door, out of his house and the inherent interiority of those—or any—walls. (But always, always, in the exhilarating moment of exit, he would recall his excitement, as a boy of seven, standing in the doorway at Fellstree, with his brother Duncan just on the other side, calling to him to come out. Oh, it was bracing! "My best ideas have come to me out of doors," Richard Dalloway had long said.) A man of the world he was now and had been for almost thirty years; yes, a former MP (he had resigned during the past year—he would write a history of Lady Bruton's family); Mr. Dalloway was off; out; walking; walking in the heart of London, *his* London, his own Westminster.

Through Dean's Yard he strode almost whistling—a grey, misty June morning, past Westminster Abbey, of course (where, crossing the street to Victoria, a former colleague— what was his name? Arnold? Alfred? yes, Alfred Hitchens— tipped his hat). And how fine it all is, Mr. Dalloway thought as he made his way through the neighborhood he had called his own for the past—how many years? (He and Clarissa had moved there soon after marrying in, when was it? thirty from twenty-seven, ah yes, 1897, an occasion they would be celebrating that very evening.) How free he felt, he reflected (for he was still, somewhat, in the interior mode, inside himself), how light and able to enjoy it all, to embrace it and take it all in for the first time in—had a year really passed? This was, he felt now, his chance for a new beginning.

Pay attention, he told himself as he walked. What was it Blitzer had advised? (For he did not have to see Dr. William Bradshaw, whom neither he nor Clarissa liked or trusted—and who, in fact, Clarissa had said was a beast. For she would never forgive him, she said—coming to her party several years back just hours after that poor young man, his patient, had killed himself; and then announcing it at her party! So they had found Blitzer—"Blitzer-not-Bradshaw," Clarissa called him.) Exercise. Fresh air. That was what Blitzer had prescribed. And to notice things outside of oneself: notice the park, the trees, the grass, the feel and the smell of the morning air ("take exercise; oxygenate yourself"), the sounds of the city, that building. Observe everything (Richard Dalloway told himself now)—for this is life, and it does not last.

And then there was the party to consider, the party that very night; he should turn his mind to that. It had struck him several months ago that Clarissa had always been the one to give parties (for she understood), and he thought it was time somebody gave a party for her, *particularly* now, on the occasion of their thirtieth wedding anniversary, and at a time when he was worried about her heart—an hour's rest every day after lunch had been advised. And so he had decided to do it, to give a party for her, for their thirtieth anniversary. But then he had immediately wondered how on earth one gave a party? He hadn't the foggiest; he would ask his sisters, Edith would know, she would help him. And so he had.

It was splendid—his particular idea, his vision for the party. In his more grandiose moments, which had been few and far between during the past year, he thought of it as the perfect union of man and nature; or, at the very least, when he was not feeling so grand, it was simply a marvelous, lucky confluence. But how it would come off now rested almost exclusively on the weather and whether or not it would clear. ("Whether the weather," he thought he had heard someone say.) It was not looking good, particularly in London; but he had bought up two cars of the special trains that were being run, which *was* terribly expensive but, he hoped, worth it in the end. And he had read in the morning *Times* that Sir Frank Dyson, the Astronomer Royal, had said about the all-important weather: "I shall go to bed hopeful." And so he, too, would hope for the best.

But almost immediately another of Richard Dalloway's concerns invaded his mind: how would it go, his being around so many people at once, with his nerves so recently shot and frayed and still somewhat raw? Clarissa had always handled things. Would he be able to cope with it all—the demands, the attention, the stimulation? And would people know about him; would they know his secret? Or would he merely spend the entire time paralyzed with the fear that they knew?

Trying to heed his own command to pay attention, Mr.

Dalloway now noticed a young mother and her two chubby-kneed sons sitting on a bench in the park. The mother herself appeared frightfully young and pale and waif-like; and both boys had to be less than five. Looking at them sitting on the bench dressed in matching navy blue suits, kicking their feet together and giggling as a duck defecated in front of them, their white teeth a milky blue in that light, it was all he could do to stay on the path; all he could do to keep himself from wavering, from falling off, into the abyss, from collapsing in a heap, right then and there. Of course the mere configuration—two young boys so close together in age—reminded him powerfully of Duncan and himself. But not only that: he had always wished he and Clarissa had had a boy—a son or sons; but after Elizabeth was born it wasn't possible. He walked on.

Still a handsome man, thought the wealthy widow Stella Bowles, a Westminster neighbour, as she spotted Richard Dalloway walking along a path in Green Park; a strapping specimen of a man, really. Must be in his mid-fifties by now, she reasoned; but he looks at least ten years younger, noticing that he hadn't yet gone white, just grey at the temples, which, people said, was distinguished. Always did take care of himself; he reminded her of a country gentleman, he did; a country gentleman just returned home from fox-hunting.

"Will we see you at the party?" he called to her across the surrounding din of traffic—omnibuses, motor cars, vans, taxi cabs. They were on separate, distant paths, and she couldn't possibly risk the damp grass with her white shoes; so she nodded and answered "yes," that "they" would see her. Though truth be told (now she looked away from him), truth be told she would rather *not* go, though she knew it was something special; knew that Richard himself and not Clarissa was giving the party (she had never cared much for Clarissa—she was too tinselly); and so go she supposed she must (her George would have wanted it). It was a bit of a surprise, this party—the invitation saying merely to meet at the entrance of King's Cross Station at nine-thirty that evening. *Most* curious. And quite uncharacteristic of him too, she thought; what *did* he have in mind? But go she would, to King's Cross, at nine-thirty, to their party—out of respect and admiration and, yes, something of an eye for Richard Dalloway (she turned back to look at him a final time as he proceeded up the path). How the world loves such a man, she thought, noticing the spring in his walk. The world loves such a man and it is his, the world is his.

Jolly to be recognised, Mr. Dalloway mused, noticing how the ducks in the pond seemed to glide across the surface of the water (he saw something of Clarissa in them); to see and be seen by those one knows (but did one know anyone, really?); to have recognition. But then the dark cloud raced across his mind again, obscuring brighter thoughts: *If she, Stella Bowles, only knew the truth. If she only knew.* It was one of the refrains or chants which had haunted him over the past year (for there were many—the truth resounds). *If she only knew. If he only knew. If they only knew.* What? What would happen? (Well, Mr. Dalloway thought now, pulling at his lapels, that is a thought I do not have to entertain, nor should I, on this historically important, this personally significant June day—a point on which he was certain Dr. Blitzer would concur. For only Clarissa knew. And she had understood.)

At the busy intersection of Picadilly, a lovely, young, red-haired woman wearing a red coat and sitting on the top of a moving omnibus stood up—clutching onto the rail—and waved, then blew kisses to a handsome, somewhat older man in a black mackintosh standing on the ground. The man received them with a smack to the side of his face and waved back. (Ah, love, Richard Dalloway thought. *Love.*)

But then a panic! Where *was* Clarissa, his Clarissa, this June day, this very morning, now, this instant (just after ten)? For a moment he did not know, could not remember. His mind raced back to earlier in the day: breakfast; Clarissa—her blue eyes blazing (still lovely in the morning light)—trying to hoodwink him into telling her more about the party (and his teasing her); saying how much she was looking forward to seeing their Elizabeth, who would be coming in on the train after noon; Grizzle's animation upon hearing his mistress's name (and Clarissa giving him a scrap of bacon from the table, which she knew he frowned upon, but that was Clarissa); and Lucy coming in and out of the room, and…? Oh yes, that was it: she had said she had an appointment with Dolly Lansdown, her new dressmaker, in Bloomsbury; then lunch in Mayfair with Lady Hosford.

Yes, now he remembered, for she had said, too, that perhaps their paths would cross that morning, perhaps they would run into each other; and he had taken her hand and said that he would like that (for they had grown closer in the past year). And then together, at Clarissa's instigation and with her encouragement, they had set about remembering those many, many years ago when they had first come in to London together.

Was it sentimental to be thinking of the past? he had wondered aloud. Perhaps. But Clarissa said it was only appropriate, only right, on their anniversary. And what fun it had been (Clarissa said), coming in to London together. What a treat. It was one of the things which had drawn them together from the beginning—both of them raised in the country, rarely brought to London: the Parrys had taken Clarissa and her sister Sylvia to Kensington Gardens once in the spring to see Queen Victoria, she said; and his parents had brought in their brood— the four girls, and him and Duncan, on the very same occasion (for he could still remember Duncan, a year younger than he was—four at the time—standing in the lush grass, pointing and saying, "Look, Dickie. The Queen's fat!" How they had laughed. But oh, how their father had reprimanded them afterwards: "Such disrespect for Her Majesty. Really. Well, I won't have it"). Had they met then, as children, that day in Kensington Gardens—she and Richard? Clarissa often wondered aloud. It was possible. But then, and still today, they had that thrill for, that appreciation of the city which only those not raised there could have.

How they loved it. Adored it, really. And they had shared that adoration, which appeared to double, to be a looking-glass image of their growing love for one another, so that the words "London" and "The Dalloways" seemed to join hands and dance. But nearing Bond Street—he had just passed St. James's—Mr. Dalloway was saddened by the realisation that it was now most unlikely that his and Clarissa's paths *would* cross that morning; for he was almost there. Perhaps they would meet on his return, he thought. He would like that. And he felt he needed it, to see her. For he had grown less sure of himself over the past year; had been shaken to his very core; every-thing, absolutely everything that he had ever known—beliefs, ideas, thoughts, feelings—all had been thrown off. But it would be all right, he reassured himself now—relaxation was the key, Dr. Blitzer had said: his and Clarissa's paths were inextricably crossed, mixed. There was a connecting thread between them which stretched as far away as one had to go from the other, a thread which not only connected them, that very moment and forever, but which also always pulled them back together from wherever they had been.

THERE'S SHAFTESBURY, Clarissa Dalloway thought as she approached it (for she had to be especially attentive to the street names this morning, as she had never before been to the home of Dolly Lansdown, her new dressmaker, since Sally Parker had retired to Ealing). But she knew the city well—there was a map in her mind; she would find it. She knew the city well because she had walked it time and time again; first with Richard, early on in their courtship, and then alone, as herself, as Mrs. Dalloway. And how she loved it—walking in London. What joy, she thought. She and Richard had, that very morning, been remembering when they had used to come in to London together. How exciting and exhilarating it was (she could feel the excitement now; her heart was racing), walking about London. (It was *still* exciting.) But then. Together. It was almost too much.

Richard had always loved Trafalgar Square best; he had said it was his favourite place in all of London—its vast, open, welcoming space. There was the statue of Nelson, of course, of whom Richard knew a great deal, having read history. But also, what was it he always said?—that it somehow took him back to the time when the Romans had landed in England. Yes, that was it. (Did he still feel that way? she wondered. She would have to ask.) And what did she love best? she asked herself now. Kensington Gardens? The Serpentine? Bond Street? Oh, it was so like her not to be able to choose *one thing.*

"There's Clarissa," the well-upholstered Hugh Whitbread exclaimed to his wife Evelyn, pausing at the corner of Charing Cross and Tottenham Court Roads and watching the figure of Clarissa Dalloway proceed down the latter. They had known each other since they were children. And didn't she look marvelous, strolling along (he thought to himself); the very picture of June—all in yellow like a parakeet (and the yellow in such stark contrast to the grey day, so that she presented quite the silhouette), wearing a feathered yellow hat and carrying herself so upright. Always so stylishly dressed.

"She looks well," Evelyn Whitbread said, in a tone implying insult, perhaps because she herself was not.

"Clarissa!" Hugh Whitbread called out to her, waving his hand about in the air (he was genuinely glad to see her). But she did not hear him (his spirits fell). It was all right, Hugh Whitbread told himself, for he would see her that very night, both she and Richard, at their party. (*What could they have planned?* Hugh Whitbread had wondered since receiving the invitation. *What could it be?*) Well, he finally had an idea—an informed idea at that, and he was certain he was right; but Evelyn would not enter into the spirit of the thing, of trying to guess; for Evelyn, who had said she would not go to their party, was not amused: "Who ever heard of such a thing?" she said. "A party that late in the evening. And at a railway station, no less. Really!"

Ah, London, Mr. Dalloway continued, now entering Bond Street (Bond Street shimmered and shone before him; a resplendent, glittering stretch). Back when he and Clarissa were courting he would pick her up at Bourton, and they would take the train in together, arriving at Waterloo, then walk across the great Hungerford footbridge. The arrival was splendid, always splendid. (The city was quieter then, he noticed.) It seemed to open up to them, to extend its huge arms and embrace them, to invite them, pull them in, like a favourite uncle does his niece (just as he himself did with his own nieces). And then once they had arrived at Trafalgar Square; well, it was—what? Splendour. Glory. Rapture. It took his breath away!

But here Richard Dalloway paused at the curb: where was it Clarissa had said she went to buy flowers? She had told him (he rummaged through his mind)...J, K, L, M (for so his conscious mind worked), oh yes, that was it: M— Mulberry's.

Mulberry's, Mulberry's, Mulberry's, he mumbled to himself—a mouthful. But there was Hatchards' book shop. He stopped and looked in the window: announcements from Duckworth, Faber (Robbie!), the Hogarth Press. What was new? Well now let's see (Mr. Dalloway took out his spectacles): something by that Freud fellow, a Viennese doctor, a psychologist, whose theories everyone, or so he had heard, was discussing at the moment—perhaps it was Blitzer who had mentioned him; rather controversial he gathered. What else? A Mr. T. S. Eliot, a poet; he did not read poetry; leave poetry, Shakespeare and all that, to Clarissa, to the ladies (he thought reflexively); the latest novel by that Mrs. Woolf (who, he thought now, adjusting his hat in the window, despite her keenly perceptive mind and—he must admit—considerable descriptive powers, had not captured it all, not all of it, in her novel of two years past: *for she did not know; could not have known*—only Clarissa knew); and the new Keynes—*The End of Laissez-Faire.* Should he pop in, just for a moment? he wondered. Buy a novel for Clarissa? Something on animals for Elizabeth (for she was studying to be a veterinarian)? Or some new history, or a biography, for himself? No, not this morning: he would continue on his way, fulfill his mission.

Mulberry's, Mulberry's, he munched the words. Pale colours at Mulberry's. Ah, there it was. He pushed through the swing doors and was greeted by a myriad of scents wafting through the air. There were so many scents and colours, in fact, that he felt submerged into an altered reality, a thick, viscous, overly pungent fantasy world; it was daunting (his nerves were still raw).

Advancing through the shop like a lioness traverses the jungle terrain, a red-handed Miss Pym (Clarissa had said to ask for her, that she would assist him) approached, asking if she might help.

Indeed, she could, Richard Dalloway thanked her, introducing himself; for he knew nothing of flowers (he looked around again—rainbows. He took a deep breath—perfume). He told her what he wanted—pale colours—and she nodded and smiled (for that was her job). Inquiring after Mrs. Dalloway (a fine lady she is, Miss Pym thought; she had always liked her), she proceeded to name the flowers as she pulled them out of the water: delphiniums, carnations, sweet peas, dahlias, peonies, anemones, roses, irises, freesia, lilac, lilies of the valley, the list went on. But he knew nothing of flowers, he said (trees were more in his line). And so he would leave it to her. They were to be delivered.

But just when he said "delivered," as if a judgement had been cast down upon him from out of the heavens, a loud noise—a pop, a boom—sounded from the street outside. Richard Dalloway and Miss Pym both rushed to the window. Had someone, someone important perhaps, been shot?

"Sounded like a cannon going off, it did," Miss Pym said, scouring the street scene, laying one hand against the side of her face. "Or a rifle shot."

A crowd gathered, descended (like crows to carrion, Richard Dalloway thought) in the direction of the offending noise.

Millicent Gordon, a healthy, middle-aged, heavily painted Bath matron in London for the day, said she was sure it was the Queen, that the Queen had been shot (and here she clutched her heart).

But wizened old Aaron Frye, who had seen it all in his

seventy years, who had been a lamplighter in Chelsea in the mid-to-late seventies; who had lost a grandson in the War, Aaron Frye heard Millicent Gordon and laughed out loud. "The Queen!" he cried, amused. He was sure it couldn't be the Queen—for the Queen was in the palace.

So they hoped, said the Hughes's, a young couple from America on their honeymoon, upon hearing Aaron Frye. "I hope it's not the Queen," said Cindy Hughes. "That would ruin everything." For like hundreds of thousands (millions, perhaps) of others who had made the pilgrimage before them, they were on their way to Buckingham Palace.

"A tyre," Richard Dalloway surmised, deflating the moment as he took in view—amidst the crowd—one corner of an off-balance motor car standing in a small, black puddle of rubber directly across the street. It was nothing. And yet it was some-thing in that it had completely exploded his composure; his sureness—both the noise and the ensuing, hungry crowd. Or perhaps it was the stimulation of the shop that was affecting him poorly, for now he felt not quite like himself. Did she really think pale colours, he asked Miss Pym; did she really think pale colours best for Clarissa, or rather Mrs. Dalloway—his wife, for she knew her after all?

Indeed, she did, Miss Pym assured him; it was a fine choice, the best (impressed she was that a man would know these things. How she longed for such a man).

Big Ben struck the hour as Richard Dalloway exited the florist shop, though not, of course, until he had profusely thanked Miss Pym (who had become positively coquettish). As he listened to the bells—one, two, three—he imagined concentric golden rings floating through the air, then settling, melting into the earth. Time was passing. Four, five, six (the golden rings floated, fell); seven, eight, nine (the rings melted; the earth absorbed them); ten, eleven. The bells stopped, and the quiet brought with it now a sense of expectation. Of anticipation. Would something, would someone, answer?

SITTING ON A BENCH in Russell Square, the leaden bells of some clock beating in his brain (one, two, three), Robert Davies noticed the lamppost light glinting off the wedding ring he had now worn for several years (though he was not married). It was his father's ring, and Davies had taken to wearing it, though it hung loose upon his finger, after his father's death (for they had been close; in fact his father was the *only* man with whom he had ever really been close—until Richard). Time, he thought, hearing the bells—it was unavoidable, relentless, irrevocable, final—time, beating in his brain that very moment (four, five, six . . .). Time, indeed (for who would ever have thought that he would be sitting alone in Russell Square in 1927, his parents dead?). Yes, time—eleven A.M. on a Tuesday morning (the *Times* was folded across his lap), and how he would spend the balance of the day he did not know. There he was, on only the second day of what was supposed to be a week's holiday: what a laugh. Well, at least he had made it out of the house, he reasoned (for the previous day he had stayed in; had been unable to go out). But now what? Paris? The library? (It was close-by.) He just could not go in to the office, for they would think him insane (nor did he particularly feel like working). Perhaps he was insane? He *had* been hospitalized—more than once; he *had* tried to kill himself. Or perhaps he should (yet again) list his assets: what it was, exactly, that he did have.

He lifted a small notebook and a pen from his jacket pocket, then flipped through to a blank page. Now, what did he have? he asked himself. Be sensible. He had taken his degree at Oxford (for surely that meant *something*). He owned a home in Fitzroy Square (he had moved there from Hyde Park after his parents' untimely death); he recorded this in the notebook. He had £500 a year until 1949 from his father (he listened to the pen scratch across the paper); there was his job (an editorial position with Faber). It was summer-time (now he was reaching; stretching and straining). And here his mind took what was, for him, an inevitable turn (and the pen skidded flat across the page), a turn towards thinking more about what he did *not* have (now he looked up into the sky as if…)—close family, love, meaning in life. His parents were dead; he had no siblings (though he'd almost had—his mother's first-born, a boy, a potential brother, had died within days after birth). The man he loved—dare he say that?—and here he thought of Oscar Wilde—the man he loved belonged to someone else. What else was there? he asked the universe—for he had read extensively in philosophy. But there was no reply.

SUCH A HANDSOME MAN, Clarissa Dalloway thought, walking through Russell Square and noticing a tall, thin, dark-haired man sitting on a bench (she patted her own hair under her hat, knowing she was not far now from Dolly Lansdown's). But so pale (she continued); like me. Pale, yes, but elegant too (she passed him), one leg hanging over the other—the lines of his trousers *just so* (clothes hang so well on the very thin, she thought, as they did on herself). And wasn't that a wedding ring she had noticed? But if it was a ring, and she was now certain that it was, then where was his wife? Had they quarrelled? Or perhaps he was a recent widower, the poor soul—sitting there on a bench, still in mourning? Oh, horrors! The very thought of it made her tremble—for what would she do without Richard? (Then, for a brief moment, as the tears welled in her eyes, the sidewalk, the trees, the buildings, and the sky were displaced, were fused into a jumbled, fractured, Cubist kaleidoscope.) She stumbled; she paused and collected herself; she wiped her eyes and then proceeded (now she was walking alongside the British Museum). There she had gone again (she thought), making up stories, stories about people, people she did not know (Richard had once warned her against it. But that was years ago). It was silly, but was it wrong? Perhaps he was waiting for his wife, she thought now. Perhaps his wife had ducked into a shop, and he was sitting on a park bench with the *Times* this June day, waiting for her. It was possible. So why (Clarissa wondered) did her mind always take that sad, that downward turn? She did not know. It always had. It just seemed to come naturally to her. Richard would say (she thought now, pulling herself together) that it was her compassion for the human condition, for he knew about such things—felt and did for the poor; the Indians (Peter Walsh was in India; in India with his Daisy). But there was Little Russell Street and Dolly Lansdown's number.

ELIZABETH DALLOWAY checked the small watch she wore in a locket around her neck—11.15. She would be arriving at choked

Victoria Station, the thought of which caused her, once again, to look out the train window at the lush, lovely landscape (that was how she thought of it); she mouthed the words to herself: "lush, lovely landscape" (for, besides animals, she also loved words). The green, rolling hills (and such a keen, intense green it was, she mused, nursed along by what had seemed an endless rain that spring—an emerald green); the cottages and cows ("cottages and cows"); the fields of wild flowers. She liked it all so much more than London, where she had grown up (London, which was dingy and dreary and noisy and so terribly, so densely over-crowded). She would live there, too, in the country, in that lovely landscape that was rolling by (preferably somewhere in Sussex), once she had her degree and was practising—for, realising that she liked people who were ill, and that animals were often ill, and remembering that Miss Kilman *had* told her every profession was open to women of her generation, she had applied to veterinary school and been accepted. Yes, it was true, though she could scarcely believe it herself. She could still remember her excitement when the acceptance had come in the morning post: "The Royal College of Veterinary Surgeons, the diploma granting body governing the Veterinary Profession," it said, had accepted her. But then came her boldest move to date: instead of going to the College there in London, right in Red Lion Square, she would go to their affiliate in Liverpool—the Liverpool University School of Veterinary Science. She would tell her parents that she had heard, from the veterinarian father of one of her fellow veterinarians-to-be she would say, that the affiliate in Liverpool was the best of the lot.

And so she had. And it was there that she would earn her degree and then, afterwards, set up her practice in Sussex. She would have a farm of sorts—her own horse (perhaps more than one), and a dog, a cat, too; a rabbit—maybe even a pig, Elizabeth laughed to herself. She would be a countrywoman (and plant her feet firmly in the earth), just as her father—to this very day—was, at heart, a country gentleman, even though he had lived in London for over a quarter of a century. (He would visit her there, on her farm in the country, and they would go for long walks across the downs.) That was her aim in life. She wanted to be solid, like Miss Kilman, not idle and frivolous like her mother. But she did so look forward to seeing them—father; mother; and her beloved dog Grizzle.

RICHARD DALLOWAY strolled down Bond Street towards, towards what? Towards whom? He had bought the flowers (and they were to be delivered); Clarissa had said she would be having lunch with Lady Hosford in Mayfair; Elizabeth wouldn't be home until later. Of course there was the party to tend to but then, suddenly, doom struck him: he was alone in the world, alone with nowhere to go, no one to turn to. He would return home to an empty house (empty, empty—the words sounded out. He had had more than his share of these days in the recent past). And so his thoughts turned to Robbie. No, he couldn't. He musn't. He was trying not to. ("I understand," Clarissa had said.) Or he was trying, at least, to limit himself—to keep it to no more than once a week. Now he struggled to look up, to look out of the cobwebs that covered him; there was Picadilly. He stopped, turned, and began walking in the opposite direction. I will just go into Hatchards' (he told himself); I will go into Hatchards' and buy that novel for Clarissa, that book on animals for Elizabeth, and perhaps a new history, or biography, or the new Keynes, for myself. Yes, that is all (he reassured himself); that is all I am doing.

Inside Hatchards', Mr. Dalloway collected himself. They knew him after all; greeted him; "G'day, sir," the clerk had said when he walked in the door. And he, what had he done? he asked himself as he looked around; he had tipped his hat in return, for he must keep up appearances.

Now (he thought, orienting himself), there was that Freud fellow; there Mrs. Woolf. *To the Lighthouse:* he muttered the words to himself as he picked up the book and examined its cover—a watery painting of a lighthouse and waves (yes, Clarissa would like it, he thought). He put Mrs. Woolf under his arm and proceeded to look around. There was Shakespeare. "No decent man ought to read Shakespeare's sonnets," he recalled having said once, "because it is like listening at keyholes...." But then it had dogged him—Clarissa herself had teased him about it from time to time; and worse, Lady Rosseter—whom he and Clarissa had known at Bourton as Sally Seton—Lady Rosseter, at their party just a few years back, had remembered it and said he had said it at Bourton, when he and Clarissa were courting. Then, there, in his very own house, at his party, she had dangled it in front of him; she had taunted him, teased him.

> Shall Time's best jewel from Time's chest lie hid?
> Or what strong hand can hold his swift foot back?
> Or who his spoil of beauty can forbid?
> O! None, unless this miracle have might,
> That in black ink my love may still shine bright.

Richard Dalloway now read on an open page. Duncan! he thought. And then he remembered: Robbie read Shakespeare! "Like listening at keyholes," he recalled his own words. And what were he and Robbie but *listening at keyholes?*

But here Mr. Dalloway tried to shake off the dusty, grey particles into which his mind had sunk. He would clear his head. He oriented himself: where was he? what was he doing? (He was breathing heavily. Relaxation was the key: breathe deeply.) The name "Hatchards'"—the actual sign out in front of the store, on Bond Street—flashed through his mind. Oh, yes: Hatchards'. Books. Something for Elizabeth (Mrs. Woolf was under his arm for Clarissa; he felt the weight of it). He supposed he would have to ask the clerk for help as far as something for Elizabeth went, for he knew little of animals (in the biological sense), and even less of veterinary medicine.

The next few minutes (time passing) would be excruciating, he knew: approaching the clerk; asking for help; listening to suggestions; and, finally, choosing Elizabeth's book and then making the purchase—pure agony. But he also knew that he could do it; for time and time again he had marched or maneuvered, riding thoroughbred waves of sheer discipline, through difficult situations. And ride himself through this one Richard Dalloway did; for he had experience at doing such things. Surely that counted for something.

Out of Hatchards' and onto Bond Street once again, greeted by the thick, heavy air, by relief, by the sounds of life itself, Mr. Dalloway stood in place on the pavement holding his parcel of books and collecting himself, drawing himself up, only to notice—once again—the noise of the city. Motor cars, taxis, and vans rode past him. The roar, the hum, of so many running motors in unison. Omnibuses whirling down Picadilly. Boys on bicycles racing by. And the people; all of humanity, throngs walking to and fro, back and forth. The orchestration of it all; a city symphony—it was dazzling, daunting. Then a loud buzzing took over, a sort of sawing sound. He looked up: was it an aeroplane? The sky was overcast. He couldn't see anything, but the buzzing continued. (He looked around to see if anyone else had heard it and was looking up. No.) Was it an aeroplane, or was it merely a fly, a fly near his ear? He swatted around both ears. The buzzing faded. Then, there, amidst the din and uproar and before he knew what he was doing, Mr. Dalloway turned and began walking *away* from the most direct route home (away! away!) and towards Oxford Street (what *was* he doing?). There was the intersection of Regent Street. He knew all too well what he was doing: he was throwing himself into it, he was nearing Bloomsbury; Fitzroy Square; Robbie!

Now he couldn't walk fast enough. Down Regent Street he flew (his coat-tails buffeted by his speed), his mind blocks ahead of him, pulling him along as a leashed dog leads his master, urges him on. He imagined Robbie opening the door of his house in Fitzroy Square, perhaps still in his nightclothes, his hair tousled (for that was Robbie; and after all he *was* on holiday). Robbie, opening the door (there was Great Portland Street); Robbie standing in the doorway...and then what? He would be surprised, yes, but would he be glad? Would he be happy to see him? Or would he be cross (as he was so often lately) and would they quarrel?

Mr. Dalloway's heart beat strong now (strong as the clock's strokes) as he approached Clipstone; that would soon turn into Maple, and then, before long, he would be there. In Fitzroy Square. At Robbie's house. Standing before his door. He would look at himself in the glass (for he was no longer young). He would adjust his collar perhaps; his bowler. He would knock and Robbie would open the door. And then—what? (Fitzroy. Now he was actually there.)

He crossed the square. He arrived at Robbie's house and looked at himself in the glass. (A piano was being played behind the walls of one of the houses. It was Brahms—a lullaby; it calmed him: he told himself that all would be right.) He adjusted his collar with his free hand; positioned his bowler and straightened his tie. Then he knocked. Then he rang. But there was no response. No one answered. No one was there to answer; Robbie was not at home (or rather, so Mr. Dalloway imagined, Robbie was just above, standing at the window in the alcove, looking down on him; decidedly *not* answering; punishing him).

A clock (Big Ben? Saint Margaret's? There were so many across London) sounded the noon hour (one, two, three: the golden rings floated), the bells seemingly hung, suspended in the thick London air; it would rain soon. Oh, it is cruel, Richard Dalloway thought—life, time: cruel. How he shrunk now, withered; how the world came crashing down on him—cymbals, drums (the sounds of an orchestra collapsing in a dissonant heap), that relentless beating (seven, eight, nine). It marched on—time. It marched on, rolled over the bystander, and left what remained—a wedding ring, the gold stoppings of teeth—left what remained behind in ashes and dust. He might just as well impale himself on the gate post then and there!

So his world quivered; so he quaked. And then, as if struggling through the deepest of mud, Mr. Dalloway turned away from Robbie's house and began walking, walking slowly down Fitzroy (it was horrible, this walking; how he struggled), unable to bring himself to look back, to look up at the window in the alcove, where he was sure Robbie was standing.

Now he dragged himself, pulled himself along; putting one foot in front of another, he proceeded. But his feet were leaden; he would never be able to make it as far as he had to go at this rate; would never be able to make it home. He would have to catch the tube; would have to abandon this summer day (this historically significant, personally important, June day)—the fresh air, the open (though murky) sky, the green, the flowers, the boys on bicycles and brothers on the bench; London itself; he would have to abandon all that and submerge himself into the dark, the subterranean, the underground, rat-infested wind tunnels beneath the city. And for what?

There was Tottenham Court Road. Not far now, he told himself. He must take deep breaths and try to relax, as Blitzer-not-Bradshaw advised. (But Blitzer, he thought now, knew nothing of Robbie.) So Richard Dalloway rode himself; so he advanced. So much effort for so little, he thought now, crossing Gower onto Montague. The law of averages was against him. Gravity was against him. Everything and everyone, was against him.

As it began to rain lightly, Mr. Dalloway, mindlessly carrying his parcel of books and struggling to open his umbrella, noticed a dishevelled man standing outside the tube station, one arm extended and the palm of his hand opened up to the sky. Wearing striped pants, a once-white, now yellowed shirt, and a vest of unrecognisable hue (it was so dirty), with a sprig of violets tucked into a buttonhole and several bunches in a shallow cardboard box at his feet, this man, this poor clown of a man, sang. He was selling violets, Richard surmised, though instead of calling out "Violets, violets," as they usually did—he was singing,

singing the same phrase over and over. What was it? (He listened closely; he tried to make it out.)

A violet in the youth of primy nature

Familiar words, and yet he couldn't quite place them. He reached into his trouser pocket and sorted through the coins in his hand; he found sixpence and five. He would give it to the poor chap; keep the violets (the flowers were being delivered). For he felt for him. He had always warned Clarissa against giving to the poor—not because he didn't want to help them— he did—but because of his belief that giving did them no good, no good whatsoever. "They must learn to help themselves," he had told her. "And *that* we can help them with—laws and whatnot." But this was different. For he felt as though he could *be* this man—turned out; no home; alone. Such thoughts had occurred to him during the past year when life as he had known it had felt so very, so terribly threatened; fragile. Now he approached the poor fellow; gave him his sixpence and five.

A violet in the youth of primy nature

the man continued to sing, over and over, as if it were a chant, all the while insisting that Mr. Dalloway take a bunch of violets (as he tipped an invisible hat).

Richard Dalloway hurried into the tube station. But now the sprig of violets he had seen in the man's buttonhole shone in his eye, burned there, causing his memory of the poor fellow's mouth to appear violet, too, to appear blue—as if icy death had already grasped ahold of him. Then came the long descent—down, down, Richard Dalloway went; down into the infinite, the dark, the cold and windy tunnel.

At least he did not have far to go, he reasoned—now seated in a car and observing his own reflection amidst the others in the glass opposite; now speeding through the darkness. The thick glass windows, it seemed, were warping and flattening and meshing his face into the faces of the others (and theirs into his): it was horrible; it was awful—to lose one's self, one's individuality; to be swallowed up like that, to be nameless, faceless, anonymous. He thought of that poor Kilman woman, Elizabeth's history tutor who, so Clarissa told him, had died last year, and who might, possibly, Clarissa said, have willed her own death, or at least surrendered her life: she'd had pneumonia for weeks and hadn't sought help (not even medication), which Clarissa said she herself would have freely given. For though Miss Kilman's smug, pounding self-righteousness was offensive and anathema to her, Clarissa told him, she had not wished her dead.

But he could not wait to get home. Home, where he was

King. Home, where he would—what? Dash upstairs to his room and throw himself on his bed? (For he would be alone.) Hopefully, he would sleep, for that would be restorative. Sleep. Rest. Blitzer had prescribed it. (Ah, Westminster.)

Out of the tube station and into the rain, heading home, mindlessly carrying his parcel of books, the bunch of violets (upside down), and with his umbrella hung over one wrist, Mr. Dalloway might as well have been treading in his sleep, for he noticed almost nothing of his environs. His mind was set, closed, locked—as he retraced the steps he had taken—how many times? thousands, probably. Towards home he trudged; towards home—his castle—he made his way, this distinguished, fatigued somnambulist.

There it was, the house—his house (or rather his and Clarissa's home); there the front door. He opened it and immediately heard noises from below—Mrs. Walker whistling, as she did, day in, day out, for Clarissa said she was Irish; the telephone ringing; clinks of silver and china; pings of glass; then a breakage, followed by swearing. All for the party, he supposed. And what did he care if something was broken? For his only wish now (and he wished it with all of his being) was that none of them should hear him and come up the stairs to greet him—particularly Lucy, for he liked her best. (There was

Grizzle, turning circles around his legs; expecting Elizabeth.) He deposited his umbrella, slipped off his shoes (which Grizzle sniffed), and then, standing in the hall in his socks, hung his coat and hat on the rack (avoiding his reflection in the looking-glass), and, as quietly as possible, began climbing the stairs.

The ascent was endless (Big Ben struck the half-hour). Climb, climb, climb (one foot in front of the other; lift, step; lift, step...). Must! Must! Must! That's what life is, he thought now, an endless series of "Musts!"—of urging oneself on, to do this; to do that; of forcing oneself to continue, to go on. And for what? For what did it all matter? This book, that law, the party—it all came crashing to nothingness in the end. To death. (He paused on the second floor landing: one flight more. The books and the violets were still in his hands.) He was old, he told himself— vanquished (the stairs creaked); he was old and tired and facing death (for he would die soon, he knew it).

He opened the door to his room, deposited the books on the dresser, removed his suit-coat (laying it over a chair), took off his hat (placing it on the dresser), and threw himself onto the bed (the spray of violets falling to the floor; he had forgotten them). Wide enough for two, it was the bed he and Clarissa had once shared; but not now; not for many years. Now they slept separately, she in her own room just beneath him on the second floor, and he in his. And sometimes at night, before falling asleep—when the house was dark, when the house was quiet—they could hear each other. ("Was Dick signalling to me?" Clarissa Dalloway sometimes asked herself at those times. "Does Clarissa want me?" he would wonder.)

How many selves we have, he mused now, unloosening his tie, staring at the blank white ceiling and feeling the profound absence he had felt in that bed—a sense of a person, of someone missing—since the first day Clarissa had left it. There was that self who slept alone, separate from Clarissa, and who sometimes heard her beneath him at night; and that was but one, a fraction of the many selves contained inside of him, of Richard Dalloway. Even the different names by which people called him: Clarissa had always called him Dick, or sometimes Richard; Elizabeth called him Father, of course. And then there were those to whom he was simply Mr. Dalloway (or Mr. Richard Dalloway); his parents had used Richie (and his sisters still did); and Robbie, finally, Robbie and Robbie alone called him Rich. And probably each of those personas held at least ten different personalities within them so that, my God—one had forty selves!

The very thought of it exhausted him. He closed his eyes and tried to think of nothing. He heard the rain falling on the roof, in the trees, across (or so he imagined) all of London. He felt his breathing slow and saw grey matter; his palms relaxed, opened to the heavens.

And then there came a visitation, a felt spectral presence which he could not say was here, in that chair, or there, standing in that corner, but which instead seemed to pervade the very room, to be part of the walls, the ceiling and the floor and, indeed, a part of each and everything contained in the room, including himself. Something was hovering.

But Mr. Dalloway was not frightened, for he knew, he recognised his guest immediately; he had received him before. It was his beloved brother Duncan (or the ghost of Duncan). The first time it had happened was in the year following Duncan's death. Richard was fourteen and, though traumatised by the loss, he had been forced—by his father, and rather against his will—to continue his schooling. During the course of that year, Duncan had visited him several times.

For it is as the air, invulnerable

young Richard had recited to himself frequently (and the phrase came to him again now) during that year, for they were reading Shakespeare's later plays (and his heart was tender), and this, from *Hamlet,* came to him, seemed to fit the situation and to make it less frightening, less painful, to him. *Now Duncan is invulnerable,* he had thought.

After that, however, after his fourteenth year, he had neither seen nor heard from Duncan again; nor, he felt, had he ever really mourned Duncan properly (for his father hadn't allowed it). Not, that is, until this past year when—under so much strain, so terribly, utterly vulnerable and completely broken down— he had finally been able to mourn the loss of his beloved brother. And it was then, some forty years later, in the soft crevices of vulnerability and grief, that the visits had resumed.

And these visits meant everything to him. Or almost everything: for they were somehow the very essence of Duncan and of himself—as the best perfumes distill the scent of flowers—the essence of him and Duncan communing. At such times he was able to continue a closeness with Duncan which he had had with no one in his life. Only with Clarissa had he come even close; Clarissa and, perhaps, Robbie.

So he spoke with Duncan; so they conversed. But not in words. Instead, they communed in a language without words; a language not known to living creatures, one which seemed to squeeze all of their thoughts, all that they felt, all of their memories and everything they wanted to demonstrate— physically—into some pure, all-encompassing and expressive means of airy communication. It was so full, so fulfilling, so...delightful.

And during these encounters Richard Dalloway always reminisced with his late brother. For he and Duncan had known each other well, intimately, better than anyone else, for thirteen very important years (the *most* important years, scientists now said). They had even looked alike—so much so that people said they could have been identical twins; and their father, or "the dullard," as Duncan had taken to calling him in adolescence, sometimes could not tell them apart. But also, and more importantly, they were always in league together (they discussed everything—talking in their bedroom late at night), co-conspirators against their father mostly ("the tyrant" was another of his nick-names), but also—at that time—against all of the women in the house, too—their mother and four older sisters. (Later, of course, after Duncan's death, Richard's sisters—Jane, Gwen, Vanessa, and Edith—took him into the fold; and he on his part, allowed it; indeed he needed it, welcomed it. Clarissa, in fact, used to say that his sisters had spoiled him, to which he replied: "Not spoiled; appreciated.")

Ah, but when Duncan was flesh.... They had shared a room from as early on as Richard could remember (as did his sisters—Jane with Gwen; Vanessa with Edith). In fact, one of his earliest memories was of Duncan and him in bed together, after everyone had gone to their rooms and the house was dark—for their father would have never allowed it, though it was completely innocent on their part. He couldn't have been more than four or five, and Duncan a year younger. During the night, Duncan had awakened and slipped out of his own bed and into Richard's; and there they had snuggled—it must have been winter, for he could remember being cold before Duncan had climbed into bed with him. He could remember being cold before, then warm after: it was his first, felt experience of the warmth cast off by the human body, and it was wonderful. Duncan's smooth skin pressed against his; the texture of Duncan's hair (silky); the cottony feel of Duncan's very breath on his skin (and the regular, rhythmic sound of his breathing); even the wispy batting of Duncan's eyelashes; the twitchings of his nose, the movements of his lips, during sleep!

Not that it was a regular occurrence, their sleeping together: it had happened—what?—three or four times all told? Four at the most (discounting the later experiences, during adolescence— which were nothing, really, or nothing all adolescent boys didn't go through, so he had heard, experimenting on one another's bodies, and thus—so it was said—discovering their own). But their room was their haven—away from their father;

away from *the women;* away from their classmates; their ghastly cousin Philip; everyone.

His fondest memories, always it seemed, were of himself and Duncan out of doors at Fellstree. One memory which ran, like the cinema, continuously in his mind, was of Duncan and him running out back and down the hill to a little stream that wound its way perpendicular to the house. It was always autumn; always blowy; clouds rushed across a slate sky so that now there were shadows, now sunlight; and the leaves of the trees, indeed the entire horizon was aflame, was golden, was red, orange, and brown, with only a dash of green remaining. Down the hill he and Duncan ran, the wind blowing through their hair; blowing them this way and that; down they raced on these riotous days to the water's edge. There they found old strips of wood or sizable pieces of bark from a nearby tree, then reached into their pockets for the small candles they had lifted from the servants' quarters, attached them with hot wax to the wood or bark, and set the boats asail and chased them downstream as they floated, propelled by the wind and the flame. Sometimes their shoes would get wet, sometimes more. But inevitably, before they had had enough, time would run out—Jessie would call them in for hot cocoa as the sky was darkening, and back up the hill they would go, grudgingly, Duncan's ruddy cheeks aglow in the afternoon light.

(But here Richard Dalloway was startled by something—what was it? He struggled up, out.... It was regular; it was rhythmic; what was it? His own heart? No, there it was: it was Big Ben striking the hour. What time was it? He couldn't be sure; he might have missed a count. He closed his eyes again; his body relaxed, settled and sank into the mattress; he drifted off.)

STARTLED FROM HIS REVERIE by the emphatic strokes of some nearby clock (for it seemed there was always a clock checking off time *somewhere* in London), Robert Davies sat up straight and shook his head from side to side as if clearing his mind. His body ached from his having sat in the British Museum for—how long was it now? Well over an hour? He shifted; he stretched; he put his head in his hands and tried to collect his thoughts. Closing his eyes (the muted sounds surrounding him seeming to increase in volume), he puzzled, he thought. He took out his notebook, his pen. And then, with the mere suggestion of writing things down, he had it! (For he now knew what he would do: merely sending a letter had not been bold enough—"Dear Mrs. Dalloway...." And he had tried to telephone just a while ago; but a woman had answered; a servant; and he had hung up.) Now he knew: he would go to Richard then and there (*Mrs.* Dalloway be damned). He knew the address; he would go there. It was that simple—

eeded to see him, to be with him. It was his holiday and he
ᵤₑ____ ₑd it—to see Richard. He had to.

Perhaps the wife will be out (he thought as he re-deposited the
notebook and pen in his jacket pocket). It was possible. He would
ask for *her* first—that was it; as if it was *she* he wanted to see. (He
got up and began walking towards the exit.) "Is *Mrs.* Dalloway in?"
he would say, posing. And when the butler answered that no, the
Mrs. was not in (or so he hoped), he would say, "Well then,
perchance, is *Mr.* Dalloway at home?" And the butler would usher
him in (for surely Richard would be there), close the door behind
them, and ask his name. "May I tell the master who is calling?" To
which he would respond, "If it's all the same to you I should like to
surprise him. We're old friends, you see—we haven't seen each
other in years. Could you just direct me to him?" And the butler
would pause to ponder this dilemma—but not for long, for (so
Robbie imagined the butler thinking) he supposed it would be all
right (now he was outside, on the steps). And then he would point
up the stairs and say, "Third floor" (for Robert Davies knew—
Richard had told him—that his bedroom was on the third floor—
the only room on the third floor, in fact).

So excited was he now with this plan that he couldn't wait
to execute it. He would take the tube.

•

"DICKIE," DUNCAN CALLED. "Dickie! Come see what Mum's brought us."

Their birthdays were so close together in time, mere days apart in the same month—August—that they were always celebrated together. And this year, his eighth, Duncan's seventh, their mother had brought them—rather against their father's wishes (so they later found out)—a rabbit of their very own to share: a big rabbit, of black and white patches and a pink, twitching nose. They named him Wellington, after the Duke, their hero at that time.

Oh, how they couldn't wait for the school day to end, so that they might rush home and play with Wellington. And before long they had Jessie's husband, Bert, build a hutch, as well as a little circular, closed-in yard for Wellington to romp in. And romp he did! Round and round he ran, his little rabbit feet kicking up dirt behind him, upon being released from the hutch and set down in his yard. Sometimes they chased after him; other times they held him close; coddled him. And occasionally, unbeknownst to everyone else in the house, they sneaked him into their room— then crawled (or hopped) under the beds with him; or they put him atop the bed, under the bedclothes, and laughed as the mound that was Wellington moved across like some great, animated mountain in miniature. (Only Jessie knew, finding all that rabbit fur amidst their bedclothes. At first she had scolded them, but then said she supposed she would keep their secret; that she had to wash the sheets regularly anyhow, what was it to her?)

"Welly," as they nicknamed him, was like a new friend— one who in no way threatened but instead heightened, increased their allegiance to one another. And that their father was against it ("rabbits are not for pets; they should run wild") made it all the better. Also now a feather in their caps was the fact that cousin Philip, despite his unoriginal, imitative wants, did *not* have a rabbit, nor could he—for his mother forbade it.

For over a year this went on, this special companionship between the brothers and their rabbit, this fun, until—suddenly, it all came to a quick and crashing end. As they arrived home from school one afternoon, their father stepped into their path. Wellington, he told them, had gone on a rampage—had scratched and bit Jessie while all she was doing was simply trying to feed him. And they couldn't have that now could they?—he had had to take Jessie to see Dr. White. And so, their father said, his brutal face shining and hideous, and so he had had to shoot the damned thing—all this while they were at school.

It was like a blow to the stomach, a blow so hard that one's breath was taken away. Richard and Duncan fell into each other's arms, gasping for air and crying "Welly," over and over again. Duncan had even lashed out and hit their father, thrashed at him repeatedly about the legs (and, though impassive, Richard had shared in this catharsis), for which the two of them were sent to their room. There they had cried all the rest of the day and into the night, going without dinner—for to imagine poor Welly in that instant when the rifle went off—the sound in his ears; the sensation he felt upon impact; his torn flesh, flying fur, and the slow, final beatings of his little heart.... It was unbearable. So they cried, held onto each other, consoled each other, and cursed their father. For they had lost something they held dear, something outside of themselves which— perhaps for the first time—they could say for sure that they loved. Now their hatred of their father only festered.

UMBRELLA-LESS, a somewhat manic Robert Davies paused outside the Russell Square tube station and opened his mouth to the rain; it was refreshing; it woke him up; it tested him. Or rather, it caused him to test himself: yes, he was sure he knew what he was doing. Standing on the pavement dotted with the wet (bleeding), blue-black petals of a violet, poised beneath the spot from a streetlight, he looked up into the fathomless sky, flung wide his arms and somehow expanded his rather narrow, sunken chest. He felt *that* good, much better—having fixed on a plan of action, a plan he was now in the process of executing; rarely in his life had he been so decisive or felt so sure of what he was doing. *On my way to Richard's,* his mind labeled the plan. It had its perils, yes, he could see that; and yet, he couldn't quite say why he had not taken such an action sooner—long, long before now.

He entered the station and rapidly descended the stairs, bouncing each time he landed. Down, down, down.... *On my way to Richard's,* he thought.

Sitting in a car, destined for Westminster, Robbie looked about at his fellow passengers. "A grey lot," he thought. But almost as quickly, he recalled that a mere hour earlier—or less, sitting in the British Museum, he, too, was grey; was downtrodden—he would have blended right in. And so he felt for them. What they need, he thought to himself (taking out his notebook, his pen), what everyone, what all the world needs, is love (he wrote it down; it was his manifesto). Just look at how it had changed him. For love (he thought) brings colour; love brings vibrancy; brings life.... One must take the plunge! (And here he almost forgot himself and sprang out of his seat as the tube hurtled along.) And so going for it he was.

THE ANGER RICHARD DALLOWAY FELT towards his father had the effect one often experiences as the result of a nightmare—

it woke him up. He opened his eyes, his red, weary eyes. He tried to sit up but couldn't; he hadn't the energy. Where was he? There was the wall; there the chair in the corner and the little Constable landscape—they were all familiar. He was home; he was himself, himself some forty-odd years later.

The telephone rang downstairs. He thought about getting up; he should be thinking about the party, he knew. How, for example, were the preparations in the basement proceeding? Was Clarissa at home (for she needed to rest)? Was Elizabeth? What time was it? Not even two; no, Clarissa wouldn't be home yet. Nor Elizabeth. Had it cleared? (He looked out the window.) It was still raining (damn!). He should get up, he knew, but he was tired, he felt flattened, held to the bed by some great, engulfing weariness. (And Blitzer *had* encouraged rest.) He listened to the rain as it fell and imagined a large cloak or tent covering London, indeed, all of London and its purlieus. But the effort of such imagining exhausted him even more, and, after a very short time, the rain lulled him back to sleep.

"No, PETER WALSH IS IN INDIA," Clarissa Dalloway said, answering Lady Hosford's question, as bird-like Miss Atkins, who had been with Lady Hosford for some thirty-five years, cleared the table and brought on tea. "In India with his Daisy," she added sardonically. "Daisy, whom I've not met; Daisy, the former wife of a Major in the Indian Army; Daisy and her two small children—a boy and a girl." To which Lady Hosford, her fat, white Persian cat—Josephine—purring in her lap, simply raised one brow and looked downward through her pince-nez (all the while thinking that Clarissa sounded like she minded, like she was jealous. For she had been there at Bourton, Lady Hosford had; had either witnessed or heard about some of the terrible scenes between them, between Peter Walsh and Clarissa—on the terrace; amidst the cauliflowers in the moonlight; and finally on that terribly hot day at three in the afternoon, in the little garden by the fountain, when Peter had kept repeating, over and over, "Tell me the truth. Tell me the truth." That they were in love then there could be no doubt. And still?).

(Leave it to Lady Hosford, Clarissa thought—for she had always been economically precise in her gestures, as far back as at Bourton. She liked that. So that's what she thinks about Peter and his Daisy. She agrees with me.) So no, Clarissa continued, he would not be at the party tonight. Sally would, yes. Or rather Lady Rosseter, as Sally was now called; living, as she did, in a large house near Manchester (she had five boys). But she really must be going, Mrs. Dalloway said, rising slowly from the table and walking into the front room; finding her coat and hat (as

Lynn Atkins scurried about to help her; for she rather liked Mrs. Dalloway, she did).

"I've had a lovely time," Clarissa said, kissing Lady Hosford on one heavily powdered cheek (how she admired great old ladies, she thought; it was because they were Duchesses. How she needed them, too—always had, since she had lost her mother when she was young; that was what Peter had said); she would see her that very night.

"Yes, tonight!" Lady Hosford confirmed, closing the door behind Clarissa Dalloway.

ELIZABETH DALLOWAY STOOD looking out at the Thames. The water was grey, reflecting the sky. She was stalling. She was not ready to go home just yet. At Victoria Station she had been so close, a mere two stops on the tube (or a short walk); and she was so looking forward to seeing them all (especially her beloved Grizzle—for, truth be told, she was of that age or stage of maturity where she still preferred animals to people). But out of the blue (she had not planned this at all), she had emerged from Victoria and set off walking *in the opposite direction*. Quite surprised her at first, but she knew; she had a mission; it was something she had meant to do for some time, but she hadn't had the opportunity. Until now. *Now.* She had to seize it.

The rain had stopped, and the air—even though it was city air—felt refreshing after the trapped, stale air on the train. She had bought a map from a vendor at Victoria, as this was not an area she was familiar with—of which there were many (for she was not like her parents—she did not know the city well).

She noticed that people were looking at her. They must think I'm a tourist, she thought, amused, map in hand. Well, I suppose I am, in some sense. For she had never quite felt at home in London; had always felt something of a foreigner (though as a tourist, she thought, I would choose to tour elsewhere—Greece; Africa!). But what was it people saw when they looked at her? she wondered now. A tall girl; dark; not unattractive ("handsome" some might say; others might say "horsy"), but still possessing some of the awkwardness of youth, a bit gangly perhaps. For she did not and would not spare herself; she was not a young woman who would gaze into the looking-glass (or anywhere, at anything, for that matter) with rose-coloured glasses. It was far better to be left alone in the country to do what she liked.

She found her way on the map: up Chelsea Bridge Road she supposed she would walk. To what? (What would be the most direct? she asked herself as she began walking, for she was good with maps.) Royal Hospital Road directly to Tite? Yes, that was it. But what was it she was looking for—Tite Street; what did that mean to her? It was a name—a street where Miss Kilman, her former teacher, had lived. Indeed, Miss Kilman had lived there at the time she died so suddenly. That was last year, while Elizabeth was away at school; her mother had tried to keep it from her, both Miss Kilman's death and the circumstances of it— the possibility (and her father had stressed the word *possibility)* that Miss Kilman's death might have been a suicide.

AWAKENED, YET AGAIN; startled by something—some loud, thud-like sound—was that the front door? he asked himself: was Clarissa home? was Elizabeth?—Mr. Dalloway sat up in bed. He listened closely. No. Nothing. It must have been the servants, he deduced; quite a lot of racket they were making this afternoon. But, he supposed it was all right—it was for the party (he must remember the party). He lay back down, his head cushioned by the plush feather pillow; he closed his eyes again and immediately thought of his visitor that afternoon; of Duncan. Would he ever get over losing Duncan? he wondered.

Clarissa had lost a sister. Sylvia. "The most gifted of us," Clarissa always said (he hadn't met Sylvia). Clarissa had watched, helpless, as a tree fell on her sister and crushed her; and it was all Justin Parry's fault, people said. It must have been horrible for her. But they had never discussed their losses, he and Clarissa, nor the effect of those losses. And yet they knew it, carried it around with them—always; they shared it; and it was, he supposed, a deep, fathomless, unspoken bond between them. Had Clarissa ever gotten over losing Sylvia? he wondered now. Could he ask her that? He guessed not. But he *could* ask himself if he would ever get over losing Duncan. It was unlikely, he supposed, if he hadn't already—at fifty-five. So what did one do? What *could* one do but remember; remember the dead and go on. That was all.

And he had done that; he had gone on; had marched through life—Oxford; marriage; a child; sitting in the House, and ... what? Robbie (if *that* was going on). And yet always—through it all, there had been an emptiness at the heart of things, a lacking, a sort of gaping hole that had not been—and perhaps could not be—filled in Duncan's absence.

What would Duncan be like now, he wondered, if he had lived? The same. Or at least that was all he could imagine; for Duncan had been frozen in time; was forever young. But digging deeper now, he supposed that Duncan really would be much the same; *would* have held onto, and continued to fight for his ideals, and thus remained young and alive—for Duncan was nothing if not passionate; indeed Richard had sometimes wondered if it was *that* which had killed Duncan (though their father, their impossible, totalitarian father had no doubt played a part).

And what would Duncan say; what would Duncan think of *him*, now? he wondered. Would he be disappointed? (What, indeed, did he think of himself?) Had he lived up to all that they had discussed those hundreds of late nights—for themselves and for the world? He supposed not. But was it possible? Was it attainable, really? Could anyone? (Duncan could—the answer came swiftly.) It pained him to think that Duncan might be disappointed in him; no, he couldn't bear it. And yet, he had to admit now, turning the thoughts over and over in his mind, that perhaps Duncan's death—in some way—had set him up for the very life he had lived; that perhaps he had read Duncan's passion (wrongly?) as a sort of cautionary tale, and had lived his life accordingly. Oh, but it was no use second-guessing.

(A seemingly muffled Big Ben struck the hour—one, two; the atoms of the golden rings, though somewhat dispersed, floated; settled; melted.)

When was it, Richard Dalloway wondered, that he and Duncan had taken on their distinct and separate personalities? For when they were very young, and up to a certain age, they had seemed quite alike, almost interchangeable. But at around—age ten or so was it?—Duncan had changed; he had become quieter, a reader (he loved the Romantic poets—Keats, Byron, Shelley). He had become introspective, yet he was still capable of surprising one by his boldness, a boldness which always sprang from thought. Whereas he, young Richard, had gone on as he always had—loving the outdoors best and spending the majority of his time there.

There were the violets on the floor with small clumps of dirt about them (he had forgotten). What was it that poor chap had been singing outside the tube station? Something about a violet in youth. That was Duncan. Yes. How he missed him. But how many fond memories he had, too. One came to him now, as if it were a kind of signal or symbol, representing something larger than itself, or so he took it. He remembered that hot summer day when the family was visiting their Uncle Gerald's. Most of the clan had chosen to stay inside, out of the daunting sun—a terrible week-long heat wave had gripped the country, but he and Duncan and cousin Philip had walked down to the lake behind the house. (It had been Duncan's idea, walking down to the lake, which he had proposed to Richard, hoping to get away from Philip. But Philip had followed.) He must have been about twelve, Duncan eleven, and Philip around the same age. Walking down by the lake, wearing their usual summer outfits—short pants, knee-socks, shoes, and shirt, suffering in the sun, sweating profusely, Duncan suddenly suggested that they seek relief by jumping into the water.

"Brilliant!" Richard had said (for he was in his element), looking at Duncan, surprised.

But Philip just stood there, eyeing both of them. "We can't possibly jump in with our clothes on. It might ruin them, and then our mums would be cross."

"Then we shall take them off," Duncan said, looking at Richard as he said it, with an oh-so-slight smile curling imperceptibly at the corners of his beautiful mouth (which Richard thought only *he* could see).

Always something of a prig, Philip had responded predictably; in fact Duncan must have been trying to provoke him. Philip's face coloured; he said he was horrified by the suggestion, that he wouldn't do it, and that if *they* did he would run and tell their father.

Duncan looked at Richard again. And Richard knew by this look, instantly, that not only was Duncan going to do it, but that he wanted him to do the same; indeed, that he was imploring Richard to join him. Then, in a flash, Duncan's clothes were off and in a puddle at his feet. He stepped out of them and took off running into the lake, and he ran until he couldn't run anymore, until the force and volume of the water stopped him, knocked him over, swallowed him up. Submerged for a moment, he then re-surfaced, his pale skin glistening in the sun.

Philip just stood there, a pillar of Victorian society, his arms crossed, waiting to see what Richard was going to do. How Richard loved Duncan at that moment. How he admired him—his bravery; his ferocity; his passion.... How could he describe the intensity with which he felt those feelings? And how could he not follow suit? He peeled off his sticky clothes (amidst cheers from Duncan) and followed him into the water. Philip immediately began walking up the hill, towards the house.

Then, instead of staying there in the water with Richard, Duncan had rushed out, running after Philip, and caught up with him. And then he ran circles around him—stark naked—as Philip continued on his way up the hill to betray them. (Later, they surmised that Philip must have given up, demoralised—for nothing had come of it.)

Would Duncan, had he lived, still be acting so fiercely and with such dare today? he wondered. Richard liked to think that he would; yes, in fact he was sure of it: for ever since he had known Duncan—when they were but small children—Duncan had always fought for and stood behind whatever it was he believed (he recalled the countless times Duncan had challenged their father). The more pertinent question for Richard now was—would he? Would he still follow Duncan's lead (for he was a follower); would he dare; would he take risks?

Or had he lost something over the years? (What *of* his career in the House? "He was fair; he was democratic," his colleagues said about him. And he *had* helped people. But because he had lost his chance of the Cabinet, and because he had retired early perhaps, a sense of failure hung over him.) Of Duncan, however, he was certain, because of his belief that instead of being merely reflexive, Duncan's actions were always intrinsic to, and a part of, his character, his very spirit. Yes. Everything Duncan had done, it seemed to him now, looking back, had been well thought out; it was done because of some principle (he had proposed jumping in the water to relieve their suffering). How he admired Duncan. It was with a fervency, with a fire, that he hadn't felt since—unless it was with Robbie.

ROBERT DAVIES JUMPED off the tube at Westminster and bounded up the stairs: up, up, up, and out into the grey, London afternoon (it had stopped raining). *On my way to Richard's,* he sang over and over in his mind. *On my way to Richard's.*

RICHARD! Clarissa Dalloway thought. *He is at home, waiting for me* (for he needed her; he had said so). But she needn't rush; nor could she resist one last plunge into the city—her city, her beloved London—before returning home; she was sure

Richard wouldn't mind. And so she walked (she was nearing Picadilly).

Traffic seemed to be quieting as the day itself wound down and tea-time approached. But no winding down for her; it would be a long night. She would buy something for the party—but what? A brooch? Long, above-the-elbow pink gloves? (For she was still undecided between her white pair, or pink, which she would have to buy; she had a passion for gloves.) And something for Elizabeth? (For, Lord knew, Elizabeth needed things to soften her appearance.) Glove shops, hat shops, Hatchards' book shop, tailors' shops, Atkinson's scent shop all flashed and beckoned, their lights—shining—reflected on the wet pavement.

An erect, yellow silhouette, Mrs. Dalloway now entered, now merged, and became one with glittering Bond Street.

I MUST GET UP! Richard Dalloway told himself. *Must! Must! Must!* That was what life was—endless "Musts!"

Once again he listened for activity downstairs: in the hall; in Clarissa's bedroom. No, nothing. Not even Grizzle. He had a few more minutes then (for he *must* get up; *must* go down into the basement; *must* inspect the preparations and inquire about the weather—all for the party). But he wanted to remain with Duncan for as long as possible.

Would he have met Robbie? he wondered now: would he have met Robbie, and would what subsequently happened between them have happened if Duncan were still alive? (And for that matter, he wondered if he would have married Clarissa.) It was not the first time he had asked himself these questions (nor, he thought, would it be the last), these questions to which he had never found a satisfactory answer (if, indeed, there was one to be had). He thought that he probably *would* have married Clarissa, but that he would *not* have met Robbie; that it was the very absence of Duncan, and the great cavity created by that absence, which had made him yearn for and be susceptible to a Robbie; but he couldn't be sure.

But *a Robbie,* he chastised himself immediately. *A Robbie*— as if Robbie were some sort of a thing, some sort of a type or other (he thought). Really! For the poor boy deserved better than that (and he loved him). But one of the things which made him think that he would not have met Robbie, would not have wanted, needed, craved Robbie so badly, was—oh. It was....

(And here, perhaps because he was entering dangerous waters, Richard Dalloway pulled back, opened his eyes to the room, and noticed the still-grey sky, the waning afternoon light and the way that light shone on the small Constable, illuminating it.) He closed his eyes again; he wafted.

It was—and by now he had slipped into, returned to that semi-conscious state (and his hands fingered about between his legs through the pockets of his trousers)—it was what he and Duncan had done together; what, indeed, he had heard all young boys of a certain age did: it was perfectly natural, scientists said. It was what they had done together only a handful of times—exploring; discovering. How astonishing it all was to him then, and to Duncan as well; but how entirely, how purely and unequivocally enjoyable, too, when he first learned about his body—what it could do; the pleasures it could bring. And to learn this *with* Duncan (which seemed to him only right); and Duncan's body being almost exactly like his: it was bliss! But then it was over; he had got just a small taste of it; then Duncan died. Which had left him feeling, what? Incomplete? Unsatisfied? Longing for more? Yes, all of those things and then some. He hadn't tasted it again for years and years.

And what was worse was that he and Duncan had never really discussed what was happening—what they were doing, discovering, together; it was the one thing they hadn't talked about. For it was always done late at night, in their room (with the door closed and locked), under the bedclothes, in darkness and in silence. Only the sounds of their breathing (now slow and quiet, now becoming faster, growing heavier—always rhythmic), only the sounds of their breathing, and the creaks and starts of the old house, could be heard.

They made a tent of the bed sheet. And once (and only once) they lit a candle (Duncan's idea) so that they could see, so that they would have a visual image to correspond to that sensation—down there—that tingle, that almost-but-not-quite-painful feeling of a growing, a swelling, a hardening. It was shocking, yet fascinating, then, to watch—the unfurling, the stiffening, the lengthening: that something which was a part of their bodies could do such a thing, could grow, instantly, before their very eyes, could be transformed, really. And then to learn, too, that such extreme and profound pleasure, relief, solace, could be had, was right there, at the tip of one's fingers so to speak; oh, it was something! But what guilt he had felt, too, later, for doing what he and Duncan had done together. Now he knew it was all right; that it was natural, normal (so they said); but then, particularly after Duncan's death, when Duncan was no longer there, so that they could discuss it; and he, at his age, wondering if what he and Duncan had done together had *somehow* contributed to, played a part in, Duncan's death (he knew his father would have said that it did). Oh, it was horrible—the guilt! It was a wild boar (he had encountered and been chased by one once on a hunt), a wild boar which pursued him everywhere, which trailed him, tracked him, grunted at him, and flashed its teeth accusingly; a wild boar which preyed on him, running at his side, haunting him at every waking moment (and at some sleeping—dreaming— moments, too). The wild boar of guilt. He had tried to shake it off—had finished school; had taken a degree at Oxford; had married Clarissa. But no. No, it was still there. And it was still there today even, though nowhere as intensely, a mere shadow of its former self.

So Miss Kilman had died, and just like that it was over. Elizabeth thought back to the moment when they had first met; she remembered: her father had come across Miss Kilman working for the Friends; had brought her home to teach his daughter history; and this Miss Kilman had done, every Tuesday morning, for years. But Miss Kilman had also taught Elizabeth something else (she thought now); something more valuable even than history. And it was this. She had said, "All professions are open to women of your generation." Miss Kilman had told her that.

But her mother and Miss Kilman hadn't got on at all, though she couldn't quite say why. Unless it was jealousy?—jealousy on both their parts; for both, she felt, wanted her; vied for her—

for control over her (but neither had it: she was her own mistress). Jealousy and, perhaps, her mother minding Miss Kilman's untidiness so much. For she herself (Elizabeth admitted now, ashamed), she herself was sometimes embarrassed to be seen in public with Miss Kilman: she was clumsy; she gobbled her food; she glared at people; and she *was* untidy—wearing that same green mackintosh year in, year out. Elizabeth had tried not to let on; and she hoped Miss Kilman hadn't noticed. Yet she supposed she had known that Miss Kilman was unhappy—she was unattractive, overweight, always complaining about her own sufferings—how poor, how tired she was; how she had been discriminated against simply because her family was of German origin (Kiehlman was the original spelling); and how she felt, in general, that she had been cheated by life. But Elizabeth had thought that other things, higher values—political passions, comrades (sisters and brothers), Extension lecturing, and her newfound "relationship with the Lord," as Miss Kilman put it, Elizabeth had thought that those things somehow superseded Miss Kilman's personal affairs; or, at least, that they sustained her. And then there was the comfort Miss Kilman said she found playing her violin in the evenings.

There was Miss Kilman's number on Tite Street; it was a

rooming house. Elizabeth approached it—no, no sign, no scrap or remnant left of Miss Kilman whatsoever; nothing. Perhaps someone nearby, someone in the rooming house or in the neighborhood, knew her, Elizabeth thought, but then just as immediately she dismissed such an idea, for Miss Kilman, she was certain, knew no one (nor anyone her). Not really. Oh, of course, there were those to whom she referred as her comrades: fellow doers—envelope stuffers, marchers, committee members, and converts-to-the-Lord.... But what could those people possibly tell her? Elizabeth wondered now. Nothing, she answered herself; absolutely nothing. She was sure of it. And what had she expected, coming down here? She didn't know. But having found nothing, nothing of Miss Kilman, no clues, she supposed she would have to think it out for herself. She had had ideas already, coming in on the train, ideas that it was the city—the dirt, the dreariness, the crowds, the anonymity—the cruel, hard life of the city which had brought Miss Kilman to her tragic, premature death. And what did the *why* matter? Elizabeth wondered now. For it was done; Miss Kilman was gone.

And yet she lived on, Elizabeth thought; or at least a part of Miss Kilman lived on, in her, for Elizabeth considered herself something of a mix of her father (and his ancestors); a dash of her mother (she admitted); and yes, a dose of Miss Kilman (and a pinch of Grizzle, she laughed; but it was true—for she had had Grizzle since she was a girl of ten). So (Elizabeth thought now), if she were to diagram it, assigning her father a W, her mother a small x, Miss Kilman a Y, and herself the Z, it would look something like this (she pictured it in her mind): $W + x + Y = Z$.

So Miss Kilman lived on.

As HE MADE HIS WAY through Green Park (*On my way to Richard's*), just as suddenly as he had had the idea which brought him to where he was and what he was about to do, just as suddenly, all of the air that had puffed up and filled out Robert Davies's sails seemed to leave him, as—for reasons he knew all too well—he thought of Oscar Wilde (Bob Willoughby had mentioned Wilde's name recently at the office). Oscar Wilde—whose example had been so strong: what Wilde had done and, subsequently, what had been done to him, had been hammered, repeatedly, again and again, into the minds of the young men of Robert Davies's generation; he had been a mature thirteen (that delicate, precarious age) at the time. (As a young boy, Robbie had been solitary, and strange—so neighbours had observed and reported. And Robert Davies Sr. reluctantly admitted that his son did seem terribly moody—always either up high or down low, which gave him pause, was cause for concern, particularly because his wife, Robbie's mother, always a mere shadow in her son's life, an evening moth, had been the same way.)

But it had been horrible for him then—reading about the trial every day in the *Times* and having the *brotherly* feelings he had and which he had had since he was a boy, a boy who had *almost* had an older brother. Confused by these feelings. Tortured by them. *Not* acting on them (though it drove him mad). And then Oscar Wilde put on trial, pilloried, jailed; his soul killed—for feeling the very feelings he himself felt; for having done the very things he longed to do. It was awful! And when Wilde died a short time later, at only forty-six, during Robbie's first term at Oxford, it cast a long shadow over his school years; he became so frightened that the only close relationship he could form with another man was with his father. In short, what was done to Oscar Wilde had sent Robert Davies reeling into retreat—for years.

Now he became a mere shell, hollow, completely deflated— so that simply walking was an effort. No one talks about Wilde anymore, he thought, though most people know, at least those aged forty-five and over, most people of a certain age know what happened to him. In fact, Wilde had scarcely been mentioned for decades (it wasn't safe), which was why he was unsure whether or not anyone born after 1900 or so had ever heard of him. Since that time, Wilde's name had all but vanished, was but a joke or a mere whisper on the lips of the very few, at certain times and in certain places, though he supposed that there were some righteous souls in the purlieus of London who still invoked the suggestive name—"Wilde"—(with their eyes flashing, nostrils flaring). They would speak of what he had done and, more importantly for their purposes, *what had been done to him,* to deter young boys, their sons no doubt, from certain perfectly normal activity. (Some people he knew, like Bob Willoughby, a fellow traveller, had told him that things were getting better in that regard, more tolerant, but he had seen no signs of it himself.) And here he was, now with his sails torn and flagging, one year younger than Wilde at the time of his death.

He slowly made his way up to Richard and Clarissa Dalloway's red-brick Queen Anne house and ran aground before their front door. There he anchored himself; paused; tried to pull himself together. I must look a sight, he thought. He backed up, moved to the side, and peered at his reflection in the window; he raked a hand through his hair. I could turn back, he said to himself. It's not too late; it's not as if I *have* to do this. No one knew I was coming; no one knows I am here. Nothing will be lost. But with that thought Robert Davies caught himself, pulled himself up short: for it wasn't true—that nothing would be lost. Everything would be lost. He would be lost. Richard would be lost. This was his chance; he had to take it. He re-approached the front door. He rang the doorbell.

CLARISSA DALLOWAY TURNED to glance back at the stretch of Bond Street, there, all lit-up in the late afternoon—a jewel, she thought, a sapphire?—as she approached Picadilly, and looking (so Scrope Purvis thought, a Westminster neighbour who was at that very moment proceeding down Picadilly with a wave), looking, in her yellow dress, somewhat gilded herself in that light; for she was, at last, ready to go home. She was tired— Elizabeth must be home by now; she would need to rest before the party.

INVULNERABLE, Richard Dalloway was thinking at the very moment he opened his eyes. (Was that a bit of sun coming in through the window? And was it that, the sunlight, which had pried open his eyelids?) He felt rested; he felt calm, peaceful. Duncan was safe; invulnerable. But Robbie, Clarissa, Elizabeth, and himself—they, none of them, were safe. Death was always hovering; he knew it. Death compelled; death beckoned and made one long to return from whence one came—from air; from earth; from nothingness. *Invulnerable; invincible....* There was nothing he could do to protect them—Robbie, Clarissa, and Elizabeth; he could not keep them safe. Duncan's example had taught him that.

But I must get up (he thought), and that was something he could do—he could get up each day in the face of it. It was all right (Blitzer would be pleased with this conclusion). He felt refreshed, restored, returned to himself—to Mr. Dalloway, to Richard, Dick, Richie, Rich—returned to whomever he was for whichever person at whatever time or place: he could be all or any of them simultaneously (for he *was* all of them).

And so he would get up. Now. He would do what he had to do (and what was that?) Oh, yes—the party; he had to tend to the party. He would do that. And it would be splendid; he knew it would: the party would be splendid. (There was the telephone ringing.) He lay back down. For he was not young anymore, though he felt it (or rather he *had* felt young, until this past year). But he had a few more minutes, didn't he?

The sky darkened again; the rain resumed.

ROBERT DAVIES STOOD in the Dalloways' hall looking all about him and thinking: *This is Richard's house, the home he shares with his wife. I am in their house. Inside Richard's house, where I have never been— though he has been in my house countless times. In Richard's house at last.* It was a fold into which he longed to tuck himself.

So Robert Davies stood in the hall taking everything in and looking, he was sure, like a scared, matted cat dragged in from some back alley. For it hadn't worked out quite as he had planned (first off, he had lost his nerve: he simply had to put Wilde out of his mind). But also.... Well, Mrs. Dalloway was *not* in, the butler said; and that *was* according to plan. But then upon asking to see Mr. Dalloway, to go up to him himself, the butler—Wilkins he believed the fellow had said his name was— had looked at him, had glanced him over (with an inscrutable eye, so Robbie thought, though perhaps deservedly so); and then he had said no (begging his pardon), he thought not; that he thought he should get the master himself; that his master would prefer that. Then he had asked his name, the butler had. And Robbie just stood there; stunned. He hadn't planned for this. But he couldn't very well say "Robert Davies" could he? For that would have been like sky-writing it all over London from an aeroplane. And so he had said "Mr. Faber." Richard would know it was him. But how would Richard react? he wondered. Would he be furious? Or would he melt (as Robbie needed him to), would Richard melt then and there (thus proving it *had* been the right thing to do); would he be glad? So Robbie was wondering when....

The front door opened. The telephone rang. Big Ben

sounded the hour—one, two, three…. All was confusion, riot, to both parties now standing in the hall. When he had first heard the latch on the door, Robbie thought that surely it must be Mrs. Dalloway come home, and he knew she would know, would know him, who he was, the very instant she saw him (though they had never met); for women were like that—they had intuition. And he had nowhere to hide. She would know who he was, and there would be a terrible scene, and Richard would come down and say that that was it; that it was over.

How strange it is (Elizabeth Dalloway thought), returning to one's home after a long absence—only to find a stranger standing alone in one's front hall, for she did not recognise this man at all. She thought back; she tried to place him—a friend of her mother's? Of her father's? A friend of the family?

Robbie relaxed somewhat when he saw the young girl come in through the door and close it behind her. He guessed she must be the one child; the daughter, he couldn't recall the name.

"Hello," she said, smiling politely (if also warily, Robbie thought. Warily and awkwardly).

But before he could respond, there was a small dog, a fox-terrier, he thought. "Grizzle!" Elizabeth exclaimed. Her beloved Grizzle—dancing all about her; jumping up on her legs; licking at the hand she reached down to him. She picked him up.

"I'm here to see your father," Robbie offered, thinking that he should say *something* to try put the girl at ease.

But she did not reply, preoccupied as she was with her dog. She merely smiled, nodded, then returned her attention to the dog (now he was licking her face) and advanced further into the house, further than he was allowed to go.

What was taking Richard so long? he wondered, continuing to look about (he would memorise it; every inch of it. Then later he would write it all down in his notebook). There was the telephone on the hall table. A telephone pad for messages (and a message very carefully printed out). A wire sat beside it unopened. And this?—a square card set atop an envelope. Ivory-coloured; embossed with night-black ink. What was it? Some sort of an invitation? He picked it up. He read:

> *M*r. and Mrs. Richard Dalloway
> *invite you to celebrate their*
> *30th wedding anniversary*
> *28 June, 1927*
> *9.30 P.M.*
> *Entrance, King's Cross Station*

How his heart raced! Then Elizabeth returned to the hall (he put his hands behind his back; he looked up at the ceiling, feigning casualness; he tried to calm himself). She stood there. She looked at him. She smiled again, then took off her coat and hat, and hung them on the rack (he slipped the invitation into his jacket pocket). It was awkward. *She* was awkward. You would think she might at least introduce herself.

The dog saved him again. There he came, running in circles about her legs; barking in little yaps.

"I'm Elizabeth," she held out her hand. "Elizabeth Dalloway." But oh how she hated this, this having to extend one's hand and say who one was. She would much prefer to be left alone in the country.

"Yes," he said, taking her hand and clearing his throat. "Mr. Faber," he said, and immediately thought that he should have used a Christian name as well. "Fff...Frank Faber," he added. "Here to see your father (oh, he had said that already, hadn't he?) The butler's gone for him."

Now both of them looked up the stairs, and it was there that their minds met—for both were hoping for the same thing, for Richard Dalloway to appear, then, there, on the staircase. Robbie wondered if this Elizabeth could detect his nervousness. Then she left the room again, and he too decided to seize the opportunity to take leave (Richard would know he had been there; that it had been him. For this was too much. It had been a mistake).

He quickly opened the door, quietly closed it behind him, and hurriedly made his way along the front path, walking in the direction of Victoria.

Now that he had escaped; now that the danger was over, he could think again. Oh, but it was too painful to think. He had been in Richard's house, had seen something of Richard's life with his wife and daughter, this Elizabeth. It was a life he was excluded from, peripheral to. Richard is a "we," he thought now. A "we"— sanctioned by marriage, by society. When he looks around his house (Robbie thought), his wife reflects him back; or Elizabeth does; or the servants. But when I (disparate I) look around my house, no one is there: even the looking-glass is empty. It was awful.

He had made a terrible mistake, going to Richard's, he saw that now. Not for Richard so much, but for himself, was it a mistake; for it had shaken him to the core. He was tempted to take out his notebook right then and there; it was his impulse, but he resisted. There wasn't time. He had to get away. And besides, what would he write? (He imagined the notes, upon which he would later expound: "Dean's Yard. The Dalloways'. Thoughts of Wilde. Plan foiled. Elizabeth. The invitation.")

And here he reached into his pocket and took out the square, ivory-coloured card. Reading it again made his heart beat too fast; made it flutter. Thirty years! He hadn't known, hadn't even considered it. Which only served to remind him, to make him confront this fact: there was a whole side of Richard's life, and indeed of Richard himself, that he did not know.

Isn't that the gentleman I saw this morning in Russell Square? Clarissa Dalloway asked herself walking through Dean's Yard. That handsome man, so pale and thin, sitting alone on the bench? She was almost certain that it was. Odd, a city as big as London, and yet it happened to her all the time—seeing people—men, women, even children—seeing people she did not know more than once in the course of a single day (so that one almost felt that one—somehow—knew them). Perhaps it was because she was out and about so much? But oh, he looked horrible, distraught, poor thing—dragging himself along like that. So then she had been right—he *had* lost his wife, to divorce or death (most probably the latter); yes, she was sure he was a widower, just come from the Abbey. Poor man (she thought). Poor, poor man. But this made her want to rush home even faster; to see Richard again; to see Elizabeth; to be safe in their home. Safe!

·

RICHARD DALLOWAY SAT UP at last. He stood. He bent over and picked up the spray of violets (he would have Lucy clean up the dirt) and set them down again, on the windowsill. Then he looked out the window—the rain had stopped. That was good for the party, he supposed. Even if it didn't clear, there not being rain would be a plus for the party. He would go down now, descend into the basement, and inspect the preparations; he would ring King's Cross Station—for Edith had provided him with a check-list of things he should do on the very day of the party.

DECIDING THAT NEITHER her mother nor her father was at home (which, she thought, *was* indeed odd), Elizabeth walked through the French doors out into the back yard with Grizzle in tow. There it was—the same small, city garden she had known all her life: the brick wall; the tree; the lawn chairs—the Dalloways' little patch of nature against this grey, grimy backdrop—the city (she peered over the brick wall). How her father had stood it all these years she could not say. By going to Fellstree as often as possible, she supposed. There was scarcely enough room for a small dog like Grizzle, she thought, let alone a whole family (not to mention, Elizabeth thought, horses and dogs and cats and rabbits).

·

CLARISSA DALLOWAY ARRIVED HOME visibly shaken. She opened the door, entered the hall, paused and stood in the threshold for a moment with the door still open. There! She was safe; safe in her own home. But it was a lie, she was not safe; she knew it. Safety was a lie. No one was safe.

Oh, but what was the source of this sudden, profound unhappiness? she wondered. She reviewed the day; no, nothing until—that was it. It was that man; the widower (she thought, closing the door). He had got her thinking about losing Richard; about death; about dying. So Richard would die, and she would be left alone, alone for years and years, until she herself died. And then the days would mount, the sun would go on shining or not shining, the grass would grow over her, life would continue without a thought for her, and it would all have been for—what? (She took off her hat and gloves and set them on the hall table.)

Ah, there was Elizabeth's hat and coat. But where was *she*? Clarissa called for her, "Elizabeth!" her voice breaking somewhat hysterically, for there was Elizabeth, and there would be Elizabeth, and surely her daughter wouldn't let *that* happen to her—left alone and then forgotten (though she knew Elizabeth preferred her father).

She took off her coat and hung it on the rack, then lifted

Elizabeth's coat (for it had been hung carelessly), shook it out, and ran one hand down the length of it as she held it out with the other. She replaced it next to her own. "Elizabeth!" (She heard a door; someone was descending the stairs.) She looked down at the table for messages: Ellie Henderson had called, wanting to come to the party (the nerve, Clarissa thought). And a wire—(oh dear, who has died?). She opened the wire slowly, with a sense of dread. It was—Peter Walsh! (Had she seen right?) Yes, Peter Walsh, in India, offering his congratulations. Which plunged her immediately back to that summer at Bourton amidst the cauliflowers in the moonlight.

But then the door bell rang. She opened it. It was the man from Mulberry's, he said, delivering the flowers ordered by a—he looked at the card in his hand—a Mr. Dalloway. Clarissa nodded, smiling and taking in all of the flowers with her eyes— delphiniums, carnations, sweet peas, roses, peonies, irises, lilac, lilies of the valley... and there were more in the van, he said. She had been amused that Richard had wanted to buy the flowers himself. But now, as she stood there, she felt completely overwhelmed: tears filled her eyes and the pale colours of the flowers ran together; nor could she distinguish among the scents. Richard was dead, and she was alone—alone for years; then dead herself and the grass would grow. But Elizabeth would remember her. And Peter Walsh, in India with his Daisy, remembered her; he had wired to congratulate them; but there was that summer at Bourton when she had chosen Richard and she and Peter quarrelled. (The young man from Mulberry's brought in the rest of the flowers, deposited them—in their vases—on the floor, between Clarissa and the front door.) And then, there was Elizabeth, come in from the back yard; Elizabeth and Grizzle. And there was Richard, her Richard, still alive, descending the stairs.

There was Clarissa. ("Hello, darling," he called to her.) And there were the flowers behind her. (Efficacy, Richard Dalloway thought: that was what he liked—that he should walk to Mulberry's in the morning, order flowers to be delivered, and that very afternoon—there they were.) He paused on the landing, from which vantage point his wife appeared enveloped by, indeed almost a part of, the flowers he had bought for her that morning.

"Let me look at you," he said, thinking that Lucy and Miss Pym had been right—pale colours for Clarissa. For there she was.

"AND THERE—there at last, finally, was the poor thing's heart!" Elizabeth was saying to her father and mother as Lucy brought in the tea. They were sitting in the drawing room. The polished silver tea service now sat on the marble-topped table—shining in the artificial light. A spray of pale, pink carnations in a small, crystal vase enhanced the far corner of the table. Opposite them, on the wall, was the Sir Joshua Reynolds picture of the little girl wearing a muff.

But she didn't think the dissection of animals an appropriate subject for tea, Mrs. Dalloway told her daughter as she poured; but then immediately she knew it had been the wrong thing to say, a mistake, that it would separate Elizabeth from her—and that was all she needed. So in a flash she put down the tea-pot and picked up Grizzle, covered his ears, and added with a smile—as if this was what she had meant all the time: "For you might frighten poor Grizzle." Elizabeth laughed, her mouth open, her small eyes larger than usual, full of surprise. And Richard looked at her, laughing too, his eyes blazing. It had worked.

That was his Clarissa, Richard Dalloway thought (still laughing)—fresh; captivating. She understood.

And yet Mrs. Dalloway continued to watch her daughter: with her tea—how she held her cup; how she applied cream and jam to her scone. Elizabeth was awkward still. She was not young anymore but she was still awkward, much less mature than I was at her age. Why Lucy has more responsibility than Elizabeth, Mrs. Dalloway thought (but I must bite my tongue). Perhaps school would change that.

"You should see Lady Hosford's cat, Elizabeth," Clarissa said now, for she knew animals interested her daughter. "You remember Josephine, don't you? Persian; all white?"

Elizabeth nodded.

"Well, she's grown so old and fat," Clarissa laughed.

Like Lady Hosford herself, Elizabeth thought, for Lady Hosford was one of her mother's friends (one of many) she did not much like. There was powder caked in the creases of Lady Hosford's face. And she was always ordering her about— "Stand straight! Don't slouch!"—that sort of thing. Or saying that in her day young girls did not do this or that. Or she would very coyly ask Elizabeth if she had met any "nice young men." It was always something. Whereas she would much prefer to be left alone in the country.

"And how was the train ride in?" her father asked her now, reaching for a second scone.

"Long," she groaned, with a tactlessness typical of the young; then added: "But the countryside was lovely; the grasses were of a green so keen and intense as I don't think I've ever seen; it must be the rains. And of course the sight of all the horses and the cows grazing."

"And how was *your* day, darling?" Mrs. Dalloway turned to her husband. "I was sorry that we didn't meet up. Especially today."

"Yes," he answered, taking her hand. "I had been rather looking forward to it." But, his day? Well, nothing much, he said: he had walked to Bond Street; bought the flowers (and yes, Miss Pym had been helpful). But here he paused and called for Lucy—a petite young woman of twenty-five with pale red hair and a rosy, button-like face (small eyes, nose, and mouth)— she had come to the Dalloways at age eighteen. She appeared at his side almost instantly. With an eye to his wife and daughter, he beckoned Lucy to lean close. He whispered in her ear: would she please go up to his room and fetch the books he had left on his dresser? "A surprise," he explained. (And Lucy ran off and up the stairs to fetch his books, all the while thinking about her Paul; wondering when he might call again. He had taken her to the movies a fortnight ago, he had; they'd seen a Charlie Chaplin movie. How they'd laughed!)

After that he had felt suddenly tired, Mr. Dalloway continued, and had come home (and Robbie had called, had come to their house, he thought; but he could not tell them that). And then he remembered: this was something, a detail he could relate: "At the tube station there was this poor chap, dressed rather oddly, selling violets. But instead of calling out 'Violets! Violets!' as they usually do, he was singing, oh, what was it? Something about a violet in its youth. Something like that, over and over again."

"A violet in the youth of primy nature," Clarissa said. "That's Shakespeare."

Hamlet," Elizabeth added.

The two women looked at one another and smiled. That they shared this knowledge (especially when Richard didn't, so Clarissa Dalloway thought) must count for something.

"And then after all of that, especially our *not* meeting, I felt quite exhausted. So I came home and slept for an hour or two. And so I am now in prime condition for the party."

Elizabeth leaned over her chair and held out a piece of her scone for Grizzle, who licked it with his pink tongue. Clarissa watched; watched Richard watching (though he said nothing). Yes, she thought, she and her daughter did share some things. And then she reminded both Elizabeth and Richard that they should take care to fill themselves since dinner wouldn't be until sometime in the middle of the night.

But there was Lucy (she handed him the books). He held them close, in his lap, so that the others wouldn't see; he turned them around and looked at their spines. Keynes was on the top—he set it aside. "But before returning home I went into

Hatchards' and bought something for you both. He handed Mrs. Woolf's new novel to Clarissa, and Elizabeth's book (he had not even glanced at the title; he had taken the clerk's word for it—for they knew him; respected him) to her.

Clarissa thanked him; she had seen it announced, she said, and had, of course, wanted it; for after Mrs. Woolf's previous book…(but hearing Elizabeth's voice interrupted that thought).

"Thank you," Elizabeth said (though she already had the book at school). But what was it that her father had given to her mother? Elizabeth wondered as she searched for the title of the book in her mother's hands. Something frivolous, no doubt. Ah, yes, there it was—a modern novel. Not a classic; not poetry, not history, not science, nor even biography; but a modern novel. That was her mother. Miss Kilman had been right.

Time did not stand still, Clarissa thought as she listened to Big Ben beat five bold strokes against the grey afternoon, a death knell tolling against all of them, there, in the drawing room, as she looked at her own daughter—how she had grown—and at her husband, remembering that day at Bourton over thirty years ago when they had first met. But then suddenly she remembered: Peter Walsh had wired! Their scenes at Bourton raced through her mind, with the accompanying emotions—by the fountain at three on that hot afternoon (I am too old for this excitement, she thought). "Did you see the messages?" she asked Richard now. "There was a wire from Peter Walsh in India—to congratulate us."

Richard smiled, for he had always liked Peter. Even at Bourton with the terrible scenes, he had always liked Peter Walsh. And why not? For Clarissa had chosen him and *not* Peter. "Most kind of Peter," he said.

It was, too, Clarissa thought. *Most* kind of Peter Walsh. And that was Peter—always kind; they had known each other, what? thirty-two, thirty-three years now. All that time; yet they had spent most of it separated. Oh, but his letters were dull stuff indeed; she could scarcely read them.

"Is everyone ready for the party tonight?" Mr. Dalloway asked, for there was his check-list which said to ask if everyone was ready.

But there was no immediate reply. Elizabeth sat for a moment, not responding; then she nodded. Her mother looked at her. "Do you have your dress picked out?" she asked.

"Yes, the green one," Elizabeth answered.

Clarissa smiled, for Elizabeth looked marvelous in green; it was her colour. "Yes," she answered her husband at last. "But first I must get some rest."

He nodded. He knew: she was delicate; fragile; the doctor had ordered it for her—rest.

And so the conversation slowly broke down, so all communication gradually ceased until the parlor was quiet and empty, the three conversants having retired to their own rooms, where they would rest.

(An empty room is a strange thing, Lucy thought, as she came in and out of the parlor, clearing the tea; as if ghosts or shadows of the inhabitants of just moments ago somehow remained—Mr. Dalloway sitting here—there was his impression in the sofa; Elizabeth, there....)

But he *was* rested (Richard Dalloway thought, standing in the middle of his room and hearing Clarissa settle in just below). Indeed, he had rested most of the afternoon. What would he do? And then he remembered: Robbie had been there; Wilkins had told him amidst everything. Or rather, Wilkins had said that "a Mr. Frank Faber" had called (and Clarissa hadn't seemed to notice or hadn't heard). And so he had guessed, assumed it was Robbie and avoided going down, but he hadn't had time to think much of it (though he had felt a great deal), until now. And indeed it *must* have been Robbie— who worked at Faber the publisher's. It was a signal; he knew no Frank Faber.

But what did it mean, Robbie coming to his house? Coming to his and Clarissa's house in the afternoon; coming to his house at any time for that matter, but especially this afternoon—with the party, and with Elizabeth here? Had something happened? Or was Robbie up to no good again? Had he fallen off? For he *knew* not to come here; never; they had discussed it. I will have to speak with him immediately, Mr. Dalloway thought (both irritated by and concerned about Robbie's behaviour). But how? It was too late in the day to send a letter, for it wouldn't arrive until the following morning, and he shouldn't risk anything, especially now. He would have to telephone, that was all there was to it. Or perhaps he should try to put it out of his mind: he would look over his check-list for the party, to see that things were more or less in order. He would think about the biography he was to write of Lady Bruton's family. He would read; he would make notes.

Lady Bruton's family, he thought now, reaching for the file of papers he kept in a drawer of the small desk at his bedside for occasions such as this, when he felt like working. "Millicent Bruton," he read. (How he admired her: she had pedigree; passion....) There was the picture of the General—Sir Talbot Moore, Lady Bruton's great grandfather—holding the scroll. (He and Robbie had once discerned that Robbie's ancestors—

which included some Moores—might have been mixed with Lady Bruton's.) Admirals, administrators—the men in Lady Bruton's family had been men of action. No, he thought (putting the file aside), I haven't a mind for this just now. It was not safe, he decided, to put the fact of "Mr. Faber's" appearance at his house out of his mind. I must act, he thought. I must telephone Robbie.

He opened the door to his room and listened for sounds in the house: nothing from Clarissa's room beneath him; nor could he hear any noises in the hall. So he began creeping down the stairs (which creaked as he went), slowly, until—just as he had reached the half-way point between the second and first floors—there was Mrs. Walker carrying a wicker basket filled with folded linen napkins. He flattened himself against the wall; she opened the door to the basement (from which he could now hear noises—voices; shuffling about; china being stacked); she began whistling as she descended—the thunder of feet on wooden stairs. He listened again—no, nothing. Then he proceeded down into the hall.

There was the telephone (looking like a black bug, he thought: such was his mission; beetle-like). He knew Robbie's number by heart; he dialed it (all the while keeping one ear cocked for intruders). Robbie's telephone rang (Richard could picture it—black, sitting on a table in the parlor. He had been there when it had rung). So it rang. So he pictured it ringing—four, five, six.... (But Robbie was not there, or was not answering.) He hung up. What to do?

He slipped back up the stairs and into his room. He closed the door. He stood: what to do? Robbie could be a nuisance. And yet (he thought, sitting down on the edge of the bed and holding his head in his hands), and yet—hadn't it been worth all of the trouble? That was the question one should always put to oneself, he had learned long ago, in the House, fighting for this or that resolution: whether or not something was worth the trouble.

Now he eased himself fully onto the bed in a supine position, his head resting in his clasped hands as he closed his eyes. He would not sleep, he thought; just think. And dream. A picture of Robbie formed in his mind. Dark, handsome, elegant—that was Robbie. He hadn't changed much in the ten years they had known one another. No; Robbie wasn't aging at all as far as he could see; he was still boyish.

Then, suddenly, there was Robbie as he had been ten years ago, sitting in that dark room at Oxford where they had first met (listening intently; his arms crossed; one thin leg folded elegantly over the other). At a reunion wasn't it?—Oxfordians were always reuniting for some reason or other. Or was it a meeting? Anyway, they had met there, surrounded by class-mates, alumni—a perfectly proper, natural setting, and then they had just happened to find themselves seated next to one another at lunch. And so as one did in polite society, they had struck up a conversation; only it had soared. So much so that by the end of the day, a Saturday, when the reunion or meeting or whatever it was was over, they had walked to the station and taken the train back in to London, sitting together and talking the entire time.

And what was it they had talked about? Richard wondered now. He couldn't remember: had it been a substantial, meaning-ful conversation, or was it merely drivel; nervous chatter? No, he thought not (for now it was coming back to him): it was about the harms of the Industrial Revolution, the spoiling of the English countryside, which, they agreed, was invaluable—an important part of Britain's capital and it should be protected; and he had told Robbie about Fellstree, said they would have to go there some time; oh, and the War, of course—the unmistakable sound of a Zeppelin during the air raids, and how they had both known men who had been killed (Robbie had said that a friend of his parents', a woman, had been killed in the bombing on Kew); and all the while, as they talked, there were Robbie's blue eyes, black hair, full mouth, and long, elegant hands, flashing before him;

waving at him; beckoning him. Then, amidst this passionate conversation (and he remembered this vividly, so much so that almost the very same shock ran through his body now), then, the train had rocked, and his and Robbie's legs had touched, had rubbed together for a brief moment, and oh! it was—what?—like a match against flint. And he knew immediately that this was no ordinary encounter. His stomach churned and his mind raced at the physical sensation he was feeling, and he realised that it could very well be his undoing: the fire had been ignited. Robbie had continued talking; he was going on about the beauty of the parks in London (for he had grown up and spent his entire life there and loved London, though he, too, he said, enjoyed the country—they shared those feelings). As Robbie was saying all this, Richard's mind, reeling with the sensations aroused by that brief touch, his mind flew ahead—to clandestine encounters, Robbie's pale limbs wrapped around him; to blackmail; to Clarissa leaving him and his having to explain it to Elizabeth; to public embarrassment; humiliation in the House (there it was on the front page of the *Times*: "Former MP Arrested!"); and finally to imprisonment! He imagined all that. And yet he was helpless; for somehow—and he couldn't quite say how—Robbie had reminded him of Duncan. He didn't know what it was exactly; nor did it really matter, he supposed, because there it was: Robbie had reminded him of Duncan and he was now completely in thrall, and there would be no way out but through it.

(But now, at the sound of Big Ben striking the hour—six? seven?—Richard sat up and looked out the window. The sky was darkening, the blue now drenched with grey.)

And so through it Richard Dalloway had begun to go, feeling he had no choice, nor any idea at all (though he had many fears) about where it would lead him. It was a journey, an adventure; a terrifying but exciting (especially at his age, he had thought at the time) life-adventure.

It had started with their meeting for lunch once a month or so: that was simple; innocent; there was nothing wrong with it. If he had the time, he would meet Robbie in a restaurant or a pub somewhere in Bloomsbury, near Robbie's office; but when he couldn't get away, which was more often the case, Robbie would come to him, and they would meet, usually at Westminster Arms (for they never met out of doors, at Richard's insistence, but always at some assigned place; indoors).

At lunch, Robbie would tell him about his father—what an unusual and extraordinarily sensitive man he was, a wonderful father; how they enjoyed their morning walks together; and that he hoped Richard might meet his father someday. (There was a charming innocence, a naiveté, and an ebullience about Robbie in those days. And there were those blue, blue eyes.) A lunch every now and then was harmless enough, he had told himself at the time, only half believing it (for wasn't it significant, he had asked himself, didn't it mean something that he never mentioned meeting Robbie or their lunches to Clarissa?).

Slowly, gradually, the lunches became bi-monthly affairs; then weekly (or even two and three times per week); and the lunches then led to teas: first out at some place or other, some place convenient, but later—as their afternoons together lengthened and the London skies darkened (for now it was winter)—at Robbie's house in Fitzroy Square, where a bed was never far away; and then.... Then it happened. Then it began—physically, consummately, officially—this *thing* between them. All of this had been painstakingly slow (or so Robbie had said later), covering a full year's time, but it was beginning.

And so it had gone on for years, amazingly enough, running along smoothly, like the best of trains: he was happy with the relationship (if also torn by it); Robbie seemed happy. Over time they grew to know one another intimately; Robbie had even revealed, as he had to no one else, not even to his father, his literary aspirations. There were occasional overnight and weekend outings in the country when these could be arranged—they had managed an idyllic three-day weekend at Fellstree once in late September (and Robbie had loved Fellstree—which only made him that much more desirable to Richard). When both of Robbie's parents died in the same year and Robbie had to be hospitalised (for he had leaned out of a third-floor window proclaiming himself to be Icarus), Richard was there to help him through it, to console him, an experience which had drawn them even closer (but which, he felt now, had unhinged poor Robbie's mind; had changed him for ever). As any two people together did, they shared life's burdens and its joys. And as for Clarissa, (he had explained to himself at the time): she had left their bed (and *that* had always been terribly dry anyway). And well, as it was said—a man had certain needs. It was not hurting her (he went on reasoning); nor was it in any way harming *them* or *their* life together, for it really had nothing whatsoever to do with them; nothing at all. This little thing with Robbie was something else entirely; it was a mere fraction of who he was, a minute (though necessary, he could sometimes admit) part of himself and his life.

But then, after the death of Mr. and Mrs. Davies, there had been a change, which he had since traced partially to Clarissa having fallen ill (so ill that he was at risk of losing her), and partially to Robbie's increasing demands upon his time (this after Robbie's second hospitalisation). For now Robbie was always wanting and asking for more—obviously as a result of losing his parents.

There was a change, yes, and it frightened him, and he had begun to try to pull back from Robbie a little. Just a bit. But of course Robbie had sensed it, had felt the reins loosening, and then came right out and said that he wouldn't have it. How red his face had grown, the veins in his slender neck bulging—reminding Richard of swans he had witnessed fighting as a child, for he had never seen Robbie like that: it was horrible. Oh, they had had terrible scenes! He was living on his nerves. For everything he had seen that day on the train, essentially his own end, which had slipped so far from his mind as to have almost disappeared (or so he had thought), now loomed on the horizon and seemed likely; seemed inevitable. He was terrified.

And it was then that poor Robbie (out of desperation, Richard now understood) had first begun to threaten him—first with suicide; later with blackmail. Which led to more scenes, until finally he had had enough. And so he called Robbie late one night and they met at a bench in Russell Square. It began to rain (he remembered) as they sat there arguing; it began to rain and people walked by and stared at them! That was it, he was saying to Robbie, the gawking passers-by only increasing his anger; it had gotten out of control and he had had it; he couldn't go on—it was over! It was over (or at least he wanted it to be over, though he soon realised that he was helpless; still in Robbie's powerful hold). But things only got worse, as Robbie took to lying in wait for him, then approaching him, practically jumping him—once in the Central Lobby!

"What if someone should see!" he had whispered, completely flustered by this abominable behaviour, this flagrant indiscretion. But that was precisely what Robbie wanted, he had said—that people should see; for he would not be ignored! And then began the telephone calls at home. And the haunting about Dean's Yard (once, walking home from the theatre at night with Clarissa, he had seen Robbie lurking behind a tree).

But "I understand," Clarissa had said, taking his hand. And looking back now (he opened his eyes and glanced about the darkening room), looking back he supposed that he could, somewhat, understand Robbie's impossible behaviour and forgive him. For Robbie was alone in the world, utterly alone; alone and desperate and vulnerable, and he—Richard Dalloway, since the death of Robbie's parents—had been his brother; his father; his lover; his—what?—his "everything," Robbie had said. Yes, he forgave him. And he loved him. And he had thought their problems were over.

And "I understand," Clarissa had said, taking his hand, to his complete astonishment. The moment he had dreaded and feared; the moment that had loomed so large in his mind for years, had finally arrived, as he had somehow known all along that it would. (There had been nothing like this between them in thirty years of marriage. There was Peter Walsh, of course; but that was before they were married; and Clarissa had chosen *him*. And then there was that girl he had kissed on the boat to South America. But that was circumstantial, almost accidental; confused and meaningless.) And he knew, too, that this moment he had dreaded would be awful—the longest moment of his life (though not the worst). But then it came and went in a flash! In a mere instant it was dispersed. All because Clarissa had taken his hand and said she understood.

It was a moment which—all the rest of his days—he would never forget. Robbie had followed through on his threat; he had written ("Dear Mrs. Dalloway..."). And what could he possibly do, Richard had wondered at the time. For several days after Robbie threatened to expose him by writing to Clarissa he had actually made sure to be home, claiming that he was ill if necessary, so as to intercept any letter Robbie might send. But then he had come to his senses: he couldn't do that; it was ridiculous! What other options did he have? (For one must think things through; think clearly, rationally.) Then, if he was home at the time, he would try to get to the late afternoon post before Wilkins did, which had put him through ridiculous scenes—racing back and forth from room to room while sitting with Clarissa (she had even asked him if anything was the matter). He had also considered asking Wilkins to take the post aside and hold it, but he hadn't been able to fabricate a reason for doing so, and without that he thought it would appear much too suspicious, and he couldn't have the servants turning against him. So finally he had gone to Robbie one last time and begged him; he actually got down on his knees and cried, and he agreed to meet some of the demands on Robbie's list (there was that damned notebook!). But no, it was not good enough—Robbie was intractable; he wanted everything; he now said that he wanted nothing less than for Richard to leave his wife. And so the letter was sent; the letter arrived. "Dear Mrs. Dalloway...."

The previous August, it was; around six P.M. He and Clarissa were sitting in the parlor (she was wearing light green) when Wilkins brought in the late afternoon post, handing it to his mistress (it was almost always for her). He had been through this before—coming home early; the post being brought in to Clarissa. And sitting there holding his breath, waiting for the guillotine to fall. In fact he had been through it enough times in those weeks so that he had begun to relax somewhat, to drop his guard. And then one day there it was! The envelope in

Clarissa's hand. He recognised Robbie's handwriting. Oh! he wanted to snatch it from her and set it ablaze. And all the while Clarissa was talking, casually telling him (as she opened the envelopes, read the letters—"Oh, here's one from Elizabeth!") who had written and what they had said, almost none of which he could remember now. It was the last of four envelopes. His stare nearly burned a hole in it; he could only imagine what Robbie could have written; what details he might go into. He pictured the letter disintegrating in Clarissa's lap; searing her green dress. And then he watched as she slipped the letter opener beneath the flap of the envelope. Pulled out the letter. (His heart was racing.) Unfolded it. (He was dying before her very eyes; couldn't she see that and put an end to it!) Then she read: "Dear Mrs. Dalloway...."

Backwards, through the thin paper, he could read the words "love affair." His gaze moved up from the letter to her face. What was she thinking? What had Robbie written? He watched (this was torture!). Her face coloured; his reddened. (The letter was but one page.) Her eyes filled, and tears came to his eyes as well, and then Clarissa's face and the letter swam in circles about the room, they were all he could see; they were blinding him: Clarissa's pale, pink face and the white page of the letter swirling in a liquid blur. He waited (but not long). She looked up. She had gone white. He could see that she was struggling to compose herself; to draw herself up. And she succeeded, only he was crying now, openly sobbing; saying the word sorry over and over again, saliva dripping down his chin.

"I understand," she said (thinking briefly of herself and Sally at Bourton—how she had loved Sally!—and then of all the Duchesses to whom she had been attached over the years and how much she had needed them—needed them still, perhaps because her own mother had died so young. Then Sylvia). "I understand," she said once more, then taking his hand and looking up at him, her eyes wider than he had ever seen them.

And that was it. They had not spoken of it since. There had been times, yes, when he had wanted to explain, to talk to her, but Clarissa always made it clear that she did not want to discuss it; that it wasn't necessary; that she understood; and that was enough. (But was it implied, in her saying she understood, that he would not go on seeing Robbie? He wasn't sure.)

And so he supposed that if it was enough for her, then it should do for him, too, as he realised that, for all Clarissa's delicacy, for all her fragility, her frivolity, her what—snobbery, perhaps? there was a strength, a resilience, and even something expansive, a largesse about his wife. (He thought of how she was around young people—how she always tried to help them and how they seemed to flock to her, save—he thought sadly—her own Elizabeth.) It was because she understood.

And so it was their thirtieth anniversary and he loved her; loved her, in fact, more now than then, at Bourton, when he had proposed to her. And that was because he knew her better now, he supposed; because they had shared so much over the years (for though it had not been easy; not perfect; it *had* been a real partnership). And when he thought now about how close he had come to losing her; that he had, in fact, almost lost her, to Peter Walsh. Oh! (he shivered). But she was his and had been for thirty years. And so there was the party, the party he was giving; his gift to her.

(And now he sat up. For I must—he thought—check my list and see that things are progressing on schedule; that things are more or less in order, ready for our departure; we should leave by nine, he reasoned.)

CLARISSA DALLOWAY LAY IN BED dabbing at the corners of her eyes with her handkerchief. She was being sentimental, wasn't she?—thinking about the past, about Bourton. Peter Walsh, even now, today, in India with his Daisy, would say that she was being sentimental. But if ever there was a time for it (she told herself), this was it. And so she let her mind roam over that vast and densely populated plain: there was her father, a difficult man; and there was Aunt Helena being cross, presiding over Bourton in her white Cashmere shawl, and Joseph Breitkopf singing badly; and then there was her sister Sylvia (and the tree falling, but—oh, no, she couldn't think of Sylvia now!). And so her mind, trained after so many years to do as she asked, moved on. There was Sally Seton—in her bedroom, on the terrace; there Peter Walsh amidst the cauliflowers in the moonlight (how they had quarrelled!); and there, above all, was her Richard, seated at the table—and Sally calling him "My name is Dalloway" because he had been mistaken for Wickham! (Now she listened for sounds of him above, but all was quiet.) She and Richard. He had proposed; and she had accepted. For she knew, somehow, by the way they were together, with each other, the comfort, the solace they shared, the equality, that he would let her be; she knew, despite how much she had loved Peter Walsh once, despite how much she owed him and how much fun they had had together, she knew, as a woman knows these things, that she and Richard were right. It was really *that* simple. And so she was being sentimental. And why not? Well, there was the celebration to consider; the party; her dress.

EXHAUSTED AFTER HER LONG TRAIN TRIP and her search for some truth about Miss Kilman's life, Elizabeth, back in her old room, lying on her own bed (atop her pink spread), had fallen asleep, with Grizzle at her side—snuggled up as close as he could possibly get. And as evening separated from day and lengthened across the walls (as a hand passing over a candle will create a shadow), Elizabeth dreamt an animal dream. She had had animal dreams often enough, only this one was truly odd (perhaps because *the animal Grizzle* was so close to her—the rhythm of their breathing and heartbeats intertwined? she wondered later). In her dream, though, blue cows flew over yellow moons and green pigs circled red stars; and she, too, was floating with them, flying—over lilac bushes in late spring; over the steeple of a church she didn't recognise, at night. It reminded her of some paintings she had seen in a gallery in Paris, where she had gone with her parents the previous year—her first time (it had been her birthday gift). But what was the name of the gallery? The artist? (Her mother would know.) So the dream was bizarre, yes; it was not logical; not scientific; and yet it was not at all disturbing or unpleasant, but was—in fact—rather wonderful. So that when she woke up and felt Grizzle at her side, Elizabeth experienced a feeling of peace, of calm (there was her old wall-paper: the vines of roses she had climbed—

with her eyes—again and again as a young girl, hoping to get to *somewhere;* somewhere else). It was a sense that everything would be all right, which—with the healthy egotism of the young—she took to mean that she *would* earn her degree; *would* live on a farm in the country (preferably Sussex), with horses and dogs and cats and rabbits, and maybe even a pig!

BIG BEN STRUCK SEVEN counts (and the golden rings fell, scattered) as each of the Dalloways, in their rooms, now sat up, now thought about the party and began to ready themselves for it. While across London, located between them and their destination that evening—King's Cross Station—and under a heavy, burdensome sky, Robert Davies lurched, off-balance, walking towards his home in Fitzroy Square. There was his house, same old house (he thought), day in, day out; there was the door. He fumbled with his keys; dropped them; picked them up and struggled to place the right key in the lock (the hole seemed so small). Finally he succeeded, the door opened, and there it was, his house. It was dark (he turned on a light); there it was: the same walls he had looked at day after day and night after night, until he thought he would go mad. There was the telephone, he thought, the telephone that never rings ("a novel by Robert Davies," he thought. Or "an autobiography"?).

He took off his coat and threw it over the telephone, covering the small table on which it sat. And in that brief moment when his coat floated, suspended, in mid-air, something flew out from beneath its folds, flew out and sailed across the room onto the floor. What was it he wondered. A dove? The dove of peace? Richard wants to make peace? Now, where had it gone? Oh! there it was. Oh, that! (he thought). For it was the invitation. He wobbled as he bent down and picked it up. Then he stood again, feeling dizzy as he saw himself reflected in the glass. There was his face, swirling in the looking-glass. His face, now smiling, for he had had an idea; he knew what he would do. He would go to King's Cross. He would join the party!

AND SO—REFRESHED, reinvigorated, and reminded of the reason for his party—Clarissa (she understood), Richard Dalloway athletically descended the stairs into the basement to see about the preparations. It was much darker down there (he observed); darker and rougher—he supposed he had been down in the basement only a handful of times in thirty years. It was hot, too. Ah, but there was Mrs. Walker, surrounded by dirty plates, saucepans, and cullenders, who had spent much of her day baking ham and cheese into pastry (she said), packing baskets, and whistling. Lucy, who had been responsible for the shortbread, stood beside her, her hair pulled back into a ribbon; and several other women (for Jenny had been let go and Wilkins taken on after their last party)—hired especially for to-night, whose names he did not know (was that wrong of him? he wondered)—all packing baskets.

The women looked up at him as he approached; they smiled, glistening with perspiration, for both Lucy and Mrs. Walker liked the master, they did, an opinion they had readily shared with their co-workers. Reminds me of my Joe, he does, Mrs. Walker thought (as she had ever since her husband had been killed in the war); and just that morning, marking the calendar, she had noticed it—eight years ago to the day that the Germans signed peace. A lot of good it did her, though, with Joe dead (now she was wrapping the silver in white linen napkins). And how she hated Germans! Still, she had been glad for everyone else, for her country. The War was over.

Mr. Dalloway asked the names of the three women he did not know. "I'm Sophie," an extraordinarily tall, thin woman said, carefully laying bottles of wine wrapped in napkins into a basket. "And this" (indicating next to her with a nod of her head), "this is Mary, sir, and that's Flora."

He smiled; he told them how grateful he was for their help; how Mrs. Dalloway, too, appreciated it; and then he asked, looking at all five women in turn, how the preparations were going, if everything was about ready.

And it was Lucy, seemingly the spokesman for the group (though she was much younger than Mrs. Walker), who answered. She said that yes, indeed they were almost ready; that there were but—let's see (she counted) one, two, three, three baskets, she thought, left to pack, and then they would more or less be finished and ready to go.

"After a moment's sit down and a fag," Mrs. Walker added, at which one of the girls (Flora, wasn't it?) laughed.

Richard Dalloway beamed. It was all going so well, proceeding smoothly (and Robbie's visit was now but a slight prickle at the back of his neck). But the weather, he reminded himself: he would have to check on the weather. He reached into his pockets for coins and then, approaching the women, handed each a pound and thanked them. "Thank you all," he said as he ascended the steps. "The party will be...." will be, will be....

Will be what? Lucy, Mrs. Walker, Sophie, Flora, and Mary all wondered, for Mr. Dalloway's voice had echoed and been lost as he ascended the stairs and closed the door behind him, and they hadn't quite caught it. "Will be dead," Mrs. Walker thought he had said, which—she added—made absolutely no sense to her. But no, said Lucy, it was "will be splendid"; he had said that the party would be splendid. And Sophie thought that she had heard him say the party would be a cad!—at which point there was an uproar of laughter from all five of them. "For we've all known our share of them, haven't we, girls?" Mrs. Walker added.

So Richard Dalloway returned to his room, hearing (as he closed the door) Clarissa stirring beneath him. The excitement! he thought, feeling it now, really for the first time; the excitement of the party. But now that he was no longer immediately occupied, now that there was not some task presently at hand to which he must turn, the prickle on his neck that was Robbie's visit turned into a weighty albatross. But what could he possibly do about it? (He began pacing about the room.) It was too late for a letter. And when he had tried to telephone, Robbie had not answered. So he paced; so he fretted. And from somewhere deep inside of him an ominous feeling emerged; a sense that Robbie's visit and what it might portend did not bode well. (He recalled the events of that morning—how he had gone to Robbie's; how he had felt he could not wait to see him! He knew he must put such thoughts out of his mind.)

But what could he do? For there was the party. He must dress and they must assemble—he, Clarissa, Elizabeth, the servants, and Wilkins, the baskets, the flowers—and then they must leave for King's Cross in, what? just over an hour now. But then, as he paced, something, what? What was it?—something framed in the window reminded him.... (He rushed to the window and pulled the blind.) What had it been? The way the tree branch, or the shadow of the tree, fell across his window? Something, he couldn't say what, for sure; and yet it was horrible! Horrible, especially now—for this to happen to him, now of all times—to be reminded of Duncan the day that he died; now when there was the party. No, his mind did not want to go there. So he struggled; he concentrated, focused on the party, on preparing for the party—on what? On Clarissa, Elizabeth, servants, flowers, baskets (and oh, yes: *he* must dress), then the cabs, and then (was that all?), then, they were off to King's Cross!

WHAT WAS RICHARD, her husband of thirty years, doing at that very moment, Clarissa wondered somewhat giddily, for it wouldn't take him half as long to ready himself as it would her and Elizabeth to prepare themselves (which reminded her: she must check on Elizabeth). He still had time. And he wasn't sleeping, for she had heard him moving about. He's probably reading history, she thought. (She could picture him sitting there, or moving about the room, walking back and forth as he sometimes did when he read.) Reading history or recording it— for he was writing a history of Lady Bruton's family (Lady Bruton, who did not like her). History, she thought now, doing up her hair. People were *her* game. So Richard's game was history; hers was people. And Elizabeth's? Oh dear: Elizabeth's was animals! But just as her spirits began to flag she saw a bit of her dress reflected in the looking-glass. A flash of white lace (and her hair, too, was white). But she resisted; she didn't want to look at herself; she did not want to see herself in the looking-glass until she had it all assembled and had collected herself, so that her entire countenance and dress, the person she would present that night at the party, Mrs. Richard Dalloway of thirty years, Clarissa Dalloway, Elizabeth's mother (and so many more selves, she thought now), was whole. She had *not* called Ellie Henderson to invite her to the party, nor would she, she decided as she placed her hat on the bed, then her gloves (a glimpse of pink, matching her face). She would not, at the last minute, not this time, invite Ellie Henderson; and that was her victory!

"But won't you come with me to the party?" Elizabeth was saying to Grizzle as he looked up at his mistress while she did her hair. Brushing her long brown hair as it lay against her breast, she thought of a horse's tail; a horse's tail flying in the wind during a canter across the downs; yes, that was herself— untamed; wild—like a horse! She was not for parties. And parties were not for her. She would much prefer to be left alone in the country. But, she reminded herself, now taming the wild beast that was her hair by fastening it with a green ribbon (green, which she associated with the natural world, was her favourite colour), it was her mother's and father's thirtieth wedding anniversary and she mustn't be selfish. For it counted for something, she supposed, to be married thirty years. But could she imagine it for herself (now she saw her reflection in the looking-glass)—marriage? It was not easy to picture herself married (she thought of Miss Kilman). No, it was not easy to picture, even though Lady Hosford—every chance she got— was always encouraging her to attach herself. But truth be told, she wasn't much interested; and her mother *had* said that she was still young. And besides, there was her education to get through, which would take years and years; and then the farm in Sussex, with all the animals. And she would not let a man (for that was her fear) stand in the way of that; not a man; not her mother; not anyone!

CLOTHES WERE STREWN helter-skelter across Robert Davies's bedroom as he went about drunkenly dressing for the party. He would wear white, satin tails, he had decided at last. And why not? Why bother trying to be inconspicuous any longer?

(For what did it matter?) White tails and, and what? A white top hat, of course; white gloves. But what else? White tails, hat, gloves and—a green carnation: that was it! He would buy a green carnation—at Goodyear in the Royal Arcade (for he had heard they grew them there); he would buy one and wear it as a tribute to Oscar Wilde, for Wilde had fancied them (or so he had read in a biography). And he was feeling quite *Wilde* tonight! But then he caught himself, paused and reflected: why was he feeling so giddy? What was there to be happy about? His lover was celebrating his thirtieth wedding anniversary with his wife that very evening. It would be written up in the *Times,* he could see it: "Richard Dalloway, former MP, Celebrates Thirtieth Wedding Anniversary." Or, "Mr. and Mrs. Richard Dalloway Celebrate Their Thirtieth." Husband and wife for thirty years; one daughter; and all of their friends toasting them and celebrating their marriage, and how could the ten years he and Richard had together come anywhere close to matching that? Who would be there to celebrate *them*—at ten, twenty, or thirty years—to sanction their union, to toast and honor *them*? (And did it, he wondered now, really matter?) And did he honestly think that Richard would be happy to see him at King's Cross? (Where *was* the party going anyway?) But all of this thinking was doing him no good (he thought as he buttoned his shirt). No good whatsoever. And so he would try not to think. He would have another drink.

RICHARD DALLOWAY had turned white. He stood, frozen, in the middle of his room, one hand cupped against the side of his face, the other wrapped around his waist. He was trembling; he was in despair. All around him now there were sounds of movement, of bustling; of people—Clarissa, Elizabeth, the servants, he supposed, people getting ready for the party; while so still and statue-like was he that he might as well have been made of stone or bronze or marble. For he had just seen his brother, his beloved Duncan—as fresh and as vivid as if it were yesterday, dead. And what was a party to that? Nothing! No, he couldn't go through with it (for though he stood, stuck, motionless, in one place, his mind was like quicksilver). Why? he asked. Why now? And what had triggered it, set it off? (He hadn't revisited that scene for many, many years!) Now he tried retracing his steps: what had he been doing at the precise moment he had seen it? He was worrying over Robbie (he remembered)—what to do about Robbie's having come to the house; he was pacing and thinking, meanwhile, about his responsibilities for the party. And amidst pacing, he had turned around (for he had reached the door)—and it was then he had seen it; turning around—there it was. But what was it? Was it some shadow in the window which somehow reminded him of it? Was that it? Or (he asked himself now, sitting down on the bed), was it the thing itself? Had he, for some reason, revisited, recalled the scene itself in his mind, that horrible scene he had witnessed some forty years ago?

Now he remembered as if it were yesterday. It was a cold autumn morning. Early. He had awakened before sunrise and gone off alone for a walk before school (as he sometimes did); Duncan, as far as he knew, was still asleep, for he could see his outline beneath the bedcovers as he looked back before slipping out the door. Indeed, everyone—the entire house, it seemed— was still asleep, for all was silent. Once outside, he felt invigorated, crunching along through the grass and fallen leaves (he looked down at his boots)—for there was a touch of frost on the ground, his hands shoved deep into the pockets of his coat. The air was fresh and cool and ever-so-slightly biting. He heard a crow's call and looked up. There, in a yew tree—so black it shone blue in the early morning light; black and shining in the tree; its golden beak opening and closing as it called out, saying what? he had wondered. (Oh! to know bird language, he had thought.) Then back at eye-level, the fragile crystals of frost in the soft sunlight, indeed the whole world, his whole world, sparkled, glittered there before him. He could see his breath as he walked down the hill in back of the house to the stream, and then along the side of it. He bent over and trailed his hand in the water. Freezing cold. He cupped his hands together, drawing the water, and then splashed it onto his face. So refreshing! And he remembered thinking, at that very moment, that he could understand why autumn was Duncan's favourite season (there was a sense of rebirth, of renewal in it), though his own favourite season was summer; but really he liked them all. Then he had stood up and seen the sun; had, in fact, been dazzled by the sun—a pale yellow lemon surrounded by a luminous, even paler pink, and then the washed-out for-ever of blue sky.

He kicked at the leaves as he climbed back up the hill, sending a few spiralling into the air for a brief moment—yellow and red, but mostly dead, brown leaves, for it was mid-November. And then, reaching level ground and the yard, he had—and this he could not explain, indeed he had never been able to suf-ficiently explain it to himself (or to anyone else), then he had walked into the tool shed. It was not customary, not something he usually did, either generally or at the end of these early morning walks. Nor could he recall feeling at all pulled, compelled to walk into the shed, as if something either ominous or pleasant, some sort of message awaited him. No, it was simply—what? Chance? Fate? For there *was* no good reason (a fact about which his father was later suspicious; his father actually accused him of helping his brother). But no, there was no reason, good or bad. And so he had pulled open the door to the tool shed, heard the rusty hinges squeaking, and walked in.

At first he was blinded by the morning light pouring in through the dusty, cobwebbed windows. But then his eyes adjusted, and he saw it. There! There it was. There he was—a white, bloodless Duncan, hanging on a rope by his neck from one of the rafters. No! Richard turned away. It couldn't be! No! It wasn't possible; it must have been an apparition. He was still in bed, dreaming. The sun was in his eyes. It was a mistake. He turned to look again. And this time, taking in the scene, the facts of it, and realising, through his eyes, the truth of what was before him (which had been instantly comprehended by his brain—all of which took a mere second or two), he screamed! He ran and hugged Duncan about the legs, screaming and crying hysterically now and trying to talk to Duncan all the while, to talk sense to him, to talk him down—anything to deny, to put to rest, to counteract the horror of what he was seeing. So confused and upset did he become that before long he was trying to pull Duncan down by his legs, screaming and crying and then hitting at Duncan until he could stand no more and fell down in the dirt floor and lay there (for what seemed an eternity), looking at the dust particles drifting in the shaft of sunlight coming in through the window, feeling the dust as it stuck to his wet face. Then, suddenly, a strange calm overtook him as he looked up and recognised the rope around his brother's neck. His father had borrowed it from Uncle Gerald, Philip's father, a few days before; he and Duncan had been there with him at the time. He had told Uncle Gerald that he needed it for—for what purpose? (Richard could not remember.) And for a moment he actually considered the possibility that.... But then he caught himself. No; not that, though he was sure their father must be at least partially to blame.

Sitting on the dirt floor of the tool shed surrounded by dust motes settling in the early morning light, with his breath—white smoke—curling about his head, Richard looked again at his beloved brother. At his brother; at Duncan—lifeless. Hanging there. And again he began to sob, his body shuddering; wracked. No, he couldn't believe it! Duncan was dead. What would he do? How would he go on? Life would stop; it had stopped. He tried to get up but he couldn't. He would stay where he was, he thought, and Duncan where *he* was; and in that way they would be together. Yes, he would sit there. Sit for eternity. For what did it matter? Life had stopped.

Tears streamed down Richard Dalloway's face now as he emerged from the terrible memory (disturbed by some sound in the house) and asked himself—yet again—*why* Duncan had done it; why he had killed himself. It was a question he had never been able to answer; that no one had answered or *could* answer (he believed now, a man of his age and experience)—for Duncan or for anyone. That Duncan must have been unhappy, miserable even, was obvious. But why? He, Richard, had not been unhappy, not generally speaking (though adolescence had had its share of troubles—largely because of their father). And he and Duncan had each other. *Why* hadn't he known? Why hadn't Duncan told him that he was unhappy; why hadn't he sensed it himself, Duncan's misery? Blame there was to be spread around (he thought)—on himself; on their father....

Oh, but it was no use, Richard thought now, wiping his eyes on his shirtsleeve. It was no use trying to understand, to second guess Duncan's reason for suicide, or for any suicide (he thought of Elizabeth's history tutor, that poor Doris Kilman: had she, too, been a suicide?). He looked at the time—9.00. He must rush; he must get ready. All right, he said, hearing himself (for he had actually said it aloud). "All right! Pull yourself together." He *must* do it! First he must try to clear his mind of this horror. He would wash his face and pinch his cheeks (for he mustn't let them see him in this state, particularly Clarissa). He would dress; comb his hair; and then it was down the stairs, first to check on Clarissa, then Elizabeth, and finally the servants, to see that everything was more or less in order. But shouldn't doing *something* about Robbie also be a part of his preparations? (He paused to ask himself.) Yes, well—he would try to telephone Robbie one last time before the party, if the opportunity presented itself.

Now (he thought), examining himself in the looking-glass over the sink: to wash this horror off my face.

THE WATER DRIPPED from the tap as Robert Davies stood combing his hair in the looking-glass. Drip, drip, drip, just as a clock somewhere ticked off the seconds, the minutes, the hours, the days, and the years...(just as the hands descended, came down on and beat at the next mark on the clockface—nine, ten, eleven; and as the hands beat at him, handled him, picked at him like crows, picked him apart). And thinking of time, of the inevitable march of time (and of all time destroyed in its path), thinking about the *crush* of time (as he allowed the tap to continue dripping, to torture him), Robbie observed himself in the looking-glass, which now took him back to that pivotal moment in his life when, as a boy of six or seven, he had been halted, stopped, upon seeing his own reflection in a puddle of rain water. The moment of the puddle. He had stood; he had stared.

But he was not young anymore. He was forty-five, middle-aged. No, he was not a young man, and what he saw, at that moment, reflected in the looking glass, himself, appeared absolutely ridiculous.

And what *was* he doing? he asked himself now. What was he doing, dressing as he was, so conspicuously, so ludicrously, and planning to intrude—uninvited—on Richard's and his wife's anniversary party? It wasn't as if Richard would be pleased to see him, or that his attending the party would somehow endear him to Richard and bring them closer. No! Quite the opposite. Oh, he must clear his mind; he must get his mind right. He should *not* go to the party. Instead, what he *should* do, was to call someone for help. But call whom? There was no one—other than Richard. Certainly none of the doctors he had seen in the past, for they, all of them, he was convinced, were quacks who simply wanted his money; he could *at least* see that. But what was the name of that doctor Richard had seen and thought well of? It started with a "B." Not Bradshaw; it wasn't Bradshaw, he knew, but B.... B....

"Bbbbbbbb. Bbbb." Robbie laughed out loud now, thinking that he sounded like a bee, a bee swooping down on a honey-filled horn o' plenty, or a hummingbird—such, he mused, was his insubstantiality. But this "Bbbb," this doctor—or any of them, *none of them* would be the sweet answer he was looking for. No, he did not believe they could help him. Nor that they wanted to; not really. For theirs was a business after all (now he was seeing things clearly, he thought). And so, he supposed, he simply must face it: he was alone. He was alone in the world and he would have to help himself. He was alone in the world and all he needed, he knew—it all came down to this, all he needed, was the love of one man: of Richard Dalloway. And so he would help himself. He would go to the party!

CLARISSA DALLOWAY STOOD at the open French windows in her bedroom for a moment before pulling them closed. And as she paused, turning her head this way and that to fasten her earrings, as she stood looking out into the small garden and at the city beyond, the cool night air came into the room and encircled her, caressing and beckoning her to revisit those long-ago summer nights at Bourton where she had stood, similarly, at windows. But there was something icy about this air, these memories, too, so that she felt suddenly old and chill. How many years ago those summers at Bourton were, she thought. And now here she stood, some forty years later, at a window in Westminster, dressed in white. But what had she been doing, she asked herself now, standing in the windows at Bourton? Indeed, what was she doing now, that same person (as if time itself had stood still)? She was waiting for something, expecting something; indeed, she saw now that she had been waiting all her life, either for something more, or for someone to tell her that there would be nothing more; that there was nothing else: *This is it; this is life; this is all there is.*

When suddenly some sound pulled her back into the room, drew her inside, through the windows, back from those many years ago and into the present moment—that room, her room; *something* reeled her in. There! It was a knocking. Someone was knocking at her bedroom door. "Clarissa?" It was Richard! Yes, Richard, for he was the answer.

She hurried to the door and opened it. And there he stood, Richard—so handsome in his penguin suit (as he liked to call it). He stood, he looked at her. And when she looked back at him now she could see herself in his eyes, as if he himself were a looking-glass. And she knew what her reflection was saying; what Richard would say. And then he said it: "You look beautiful, darling. Positively stunning." And that was enough. So they embraced.

But had Clarissa been looking carefully as she stood at her open window, she would have seen Elizabeth walking about in the garden with Grizzle. She was throwing a red ball here and there as Grizzle fetched and then retrieved it, over and over again, just as she had taught him to do shortly after she first got him ten years ago. "There's a good boy." She bent down and petted his head, her green dress dragging through the wet grass and the moist earth.

A mere petting is not enough, Elizabeth thought, since they would be away at the party and Grizzle would be alone for quite some time. She would fetch some scrap from Lucy to give him. "Want a bone, Griz?" she asked him now, her voice rising on the word "bone," so that he would understand her. He did understand, and he began wagging his tail vigorously and running about her feet panting, all the while looking up at her, looking into her face, looking for the bone.

"There's Elizabeth," Richard said as he and Clarissa stood together at the bottom of the stairs, glancing past the parlor, through the yellow curtains with the birds of Paradise, and out the open French doors, into the garden.

"What on earth *are* you doing, Elizabeth?" Clarissa asked, irritated, for she could see that her daughter's hands were dirty.

"Just playing with Grizzle, Mother."

It was just like Elizabeth to be so calm and relaxed about it all, Clarissa thought.

"Come in, please, and wash up," she said. "We're about to leave." But why couldn't Richard have said that? she asked herself now as he stood beside her. Why was it that *she* was the one always having to tell Elizabeth to do this or that? But she mustn't let herself get upset; and there was Elizabeth. Oh, dear, she had dirt not only on her shoes but on the hem of her dress as well, Clarissa could see it, and she couldn't allow any daughter of hers to go to a party looking like that. (Where was Elizabeth's mind? she wondered. Had she lost her senses?—playing in the dirt in her best clothes before the party.)

She *is* terribly immature for twenty, Clarissa thought now, remembering herself at that age—how she had already lost her mother, *and Sylvia,* and how she then had to care for her father, to play hostess at Bourton and ... attend balls. But perhaps the rigour of this veterinary program will help her mature (Clarissa mused, composing herself).

But Richard really must speak to Elizabeth; she would have him say something about the dirt on her shoes and dress as if he had just spotted it himself. Yes, he, Elizabeth's father, would have to tell her that she must wipe the dirt off her shoes and try to wash it out of the hem of her dress (for Lucy was busy); and if that proved unsuccessful, then she would have to change.

But here came the servants, she could hear them—banging

about as they trudged up the stairs from the basement, then appeared, carrying baskets. Into the room walked Lucy, a happy girl—she always had a smile, and she told Mrs. Dalloway how perfectly lovely she looked, followed by Mrs. Walker (who reeked, Clarissa thought, of cigarette smoke), and then there were the three specially hired girls—Sophie, Flora, and Mary she thought their names were, yes; and Wilkins, who— resembling nothing less than a grey fox—took his place by the flowers as if he were guarding them.

"And doesn't the master look handsome, girls?" Mrs. Walker asked, winking, to which Lucy nodded, and Sophie and Flora and Mary all giggled, not feeling as comfortable or as familiar as Mrs. Walker and Lucy did. Mr. Dalloway blushed, and—smiling—thanked Mrs. Walker, and then he turned to ask Wilkins if he had called for the taxi cabs? He thought they would need two.

No, he had not called, Wilkins answered, saying that he had been waiting for the word, which now—having had it—he would do; he would call.

And then, as if the party motor had been turned on, or turned up (for it had been idling for quite some time), everyone, it seemed, began moving and working in its current, towards that end. As soon as he had hung up the telephone, Wilkins began carrying out the flowers, he could see that it would take him several trips, while Lucy and Mrs. Walker and the three girls brought the baskets out through the front door and set them down (Mrs. Walker let out a sigh), and just as Clarissa had asked, with a touch of irritation in her voice, where *was* Elizabeth? there she came, rushing into the hall, flushed and proclaiming herself *and* her dress clean (Clarissa looked at the dress and saw no dirt, much to her relief, so she smiled at Elizabeth), and Grizzle circled Elizabeth's feet, and Richard, feeling like the ringmaster at a circus, good-naturedly asked— "Are we ready? Is everyone ready for the party?" Then he took Clarissa's arm and the two of them, with Elizabeth in tow (lingering and saying good-bye to Grizzle), exited the house and closed the front door behind them just as the taxi cabs were pulling up.

The night air was cool. It was not raining, but nor were the London skies clear; instead, they had that familiar, yellow-grey sulphurous look which often presented itself on overcast summer nights. And as they climbed into the taxi cab, Clarissa and Elizabeth and—no, Richard paused, for he could see that they would need a third car. (He told Wilkins to call for it.) He would ride with Clarissa and Elizabeth, of course; Wilkins and the flowers could occupy this other one (for Mulberry's had used a van, after all); and then Lucy and Mrs. Walker, the three other girls *and the baskets* would all have to pile into the third when it arrived (poor planning, he thought, chastising himself).

But she hoped there was a cab left unoccupied in the city, Clarissa said (at which Elizabeth laughed), for she imagined many of them were being used up by their guests (or by practically everyone else in London, Richard thought, knowing that there would be quite a convergence on King's Cross this personally significant and historically important June night).

And so Clarissa imagined them, her party-goers, pouring out into the streets of London—in taxi cabs, on foot, by tube, or in their own motor cars, driving in from the purlieus or from even further out—all of her party-goers emptying out of their houses and being swept up by the momentum and the pull of the party, converging and flowing, all together, swirling around the circles and squares that were the streets of London, and then arriving (but hopefully not colliding, she thought, for the London streets *were* dangerous), so she imagined them—Lady Hosford, Stella Bowles, Lady Lovejoy (she began going through the guest-list in her mind, pictured it, saw it now on the several sheets of white paper, in her own handwriting, just as she had written it out; she saw the names and checked them off—in her mind), Lord and Lady Lexham, Colonel and Mrs. Garrod,

Hugh Whitbread, alone—always alone, for Evelyn was sick (poor Hugh), and Mr. Bowley, Mrs. Hilbery, Lady Mary Maddox, Herbert Ainsty, Mrs. Dakers, Lady Bruton (who did not like her), and Sally, Sally Seton (or what was her name now—Lady Rosseter? Sally, who was supposed to bring her husband this time, for they had not met), and Mrs. Durrant and Clara, Katherine Truelock and Eleanor Gibson (who, someone had told her, were Sapphists, which was nothing to her, for she had known Katherine since they were girls), and Sir Harry, Willie Titcomb, Professor Brierly (he always wore red socks), Prickett Ellis, (but not Ellie Henderson, she thought victoriously, pausing now and trying to remember the other names on the list, for she had not invited Ellie), oh yes, and Ralph Johnson, the Brunners, Miss O'Keefe, Lily Everit, Bob Brinsley, Mr. and Mrs. Bromley, Mrs. Vallance (another Duchess she admired), Jack Renshaw, oh yes, and how could she forget the lovely Sasha Richardson—so she imagined them all, some already there, perhaps, waiting, others poking along, a few even running late and racing (that would be Sally, or at least the old Sally) so as to arrive at King's Cross Station by 9.30.

The motors of the two taxi cabs hummed in Richard Dalloway's ears now as they sat waiting for Wilkins to return from telephoning for the third. And the humming became a sort of drone which, as they waited—and while Elizabeth was saying *something* to Clarissa about school, he wasn't really listening— lulled him into recalling where he had been and what he had seen: Duncan, hanging there (forty years earlier). And then (he thought, shaking off *that* memory) there was the matter of Robbie. He would try to telephone him from King's Cross.

But there was Wilkins coming out the front door, waving to him and then climbing into the taxi cab, surrounded by the flowers, and pale colours were certainly not for him (Lucy thought with a laugh). And then they were off, moving, as Lucy and Mrs. Walker and the three girls waved good-bye and called "See you at King's Cross!" For they felt as though they were on an adventure.

PART TWO
The Party

H

ad his idea for the party been grandiose? Richard Dalloway wondered now, standing in a corner but at some distance from the entrance of King's Cross Station (on a brief errand, he had told Clarissa), now watching his wife as she graciously greeted their guests. (There was Stella Bowles. She had seen him. She waved flirtatiously—talking with Clarissa, whom, or so Clarissa said, she did not like. He waved back.) But it was not the first time he had worried over this question about the party in the past few days; and he supposed it *was* possible— that his idea was rather grandiose (but it was too late now), for what he wanted to do, his highest goal for the party, besides pleasing Clarissa (for he still had *some* ambition, some desire to integrate personal and public concerns), was to take a group of people, his and Clarissa's friends (mostly Clarissa's, for he had not had much time for friends over the years, what with his duties in the House)—he wanted nothing less than to take Clarissa and Elizabeth and their friends and to bring them out of the drawing rooms and the parlours, out of their houses, out of doors, away from all that artifice, and then—somehow as one, as *a party* of people—to connect them, *en masse,* with the natural world, something larger than themselves, something more than merely the who, what, when, where, and how of their meager day-to-day existences, something bigger and more profound. And that something, he supposed now, was nothing less than the universe itself. So yes, maybe he had been—what was that word Blitzer had used?—*delusional*, that was it; maybe he had been *delusional* when he first came up with the design for the party—an effect of the previous year's events on his mind, perhaps? he wondered. But, he thought now, it is not over yet. (He reminded himself that he must remember to talk with Millicent Bruton about her ancestors—now that he had *all* of the papers from Aldmixton; for he would be occupying his hours in the days and months and years to come with writing the biography of her family.)

And then there was his errand. He had left the crowd to try to telephone Robbie (and to compose himself one last time before the party began in earnest), but again there had been no answer. He could see now that if he was going to get on with the evening at all, he would have to just let it go, to try to put Robbie out of his mind and give himself over wholly to the thing at hand, to the party.

And she did look lovely, Stella Bowles had to admit, seeing Clarissa Dalloway standing there; greeting her guests; nodding her head; smiling; laughing; shaking the hands of some and embracing others; playing the role she loved most and was best known for, that of hostess. Yes, she did look lovely, all in white (dress, hair), with pale pink, above-the-elbow gloves, and a matching pink hat. And that simple strand of pearls. So characteristic, Stella Bowles thought—Clarissa's all-too-obvious reference to the fact that it was her and Richard's thirtieth anniversary, for which pearl, she was certain Clarissa would know, was the appropriate gemstone. Whereas because of George's premature death at age forty-nine (the House, she was convinced, had killed him), she had been deprived of *their* thirtieth.

But Clarissa Dalloway herself was only aware of the fact that she scarcely had time to think at all, save for the spare, brief moment, amidst greeting people and shaking their hands and saying how long it had been and embracing some and catching this whiff of perfume and that glance at someone's handsome Spanish shawl or smart new hat from Paris or diamond brooch ("from Bond Street"). Not to mention, she thought now, worrying about Elizabeth, and about the party—how it would go (for a party was an offering after all), and feeling, that though it was Richard who was giving the party, though it had been his idea, its success or failure, she knew—in the end—ultimately rested upon her shoulders.

Now walking back over to join the gathering crowd and properly assume his role as host, Richard Dalloway was asked, again and again, from this group and from that (always good-humouredly) as he made his way, the question of the hour: "What *are* we doing at King's Cross Station at nine-thirty in the evening?" To which various other guests would add, looking around the busy station: "Where is the party?" "When does it begin?" "Are we taking a train somewhere?" Though just as many thought that they *knew* where the party was going and for what purpose, but they would keep Richard Dalloway's secret.

Like Hugh Whitbread, for example—he knew what was up (as he imagined most of *the men* did), overhearing the questions put to Richard Dalloway (always in a feminine voice, he thought). For he kept up with things, prided himself on it; he kept up with things and knew both what day this was *and* the historical significance of it; for he read his morning *Times* religiously. And he thought it a splendid idea, really, if also a bit far-reaching and unconventional (Evelyn had said it was pure hogwash), particularly for Richard Dalloway, whom he'd known forever.

And so they came, into the mouth of King's Cross Station and under the two great sheltering arches that comprise its body, first in droves, and then more slowly, one by one, as a clock ticks off the minutes. Stella Bowles had been the first to arrive. She had seen Richard that morning in the park, she told Clarissa; hadn't he mentioned it? (Her feathers were ruffled.) Stella Bowles, followed by Lady Hosford, wearing a fur stole over crimson moiré (in June no less) and accompanied by Miss Atkins, which, Clarissa thought, was really *too much*, for Lynn Atkins had not been invited. And what if everyone had decided to bring *their* servants along…. It would have been a fine mess. She might as well have brought Josephine the cat, too—and Elizabeth could have brought Grizzle! But there she was, Lady Hosford, in a powder cloud (Lynn Atkins scurrying along beside her), a Duchess for whom Clarissa remained grateful (they embraced), as she had all of her adult life. And I am up to it, Clarissa thought; I can carry the party if I have to.

Whereas old Wilkins, who had at first tried to announce

each of the guests as they arrived—"Mrs. George Bowles," "Lady Hosford"—just as he always did at their parties at home in Westminster, had abandoned any such hope of doing so. For there were people coming at him now from so many directions that he could not keep up, and finally—crossing his arms and giving one big "harumpf!" in exasperation—he resumed his position as guardian of the flowers, for *they* were manageable (and could be carried on to the train now, his master told him).

And Mrs. Walker was saying how tired she was of standing already, how her poor old legs hurt and how she wished they would get on with it, for it would be a long night (whereas all she really wanted now, she said, was a fag). But Lucy reminded Mrs. Walker that she was only forty-three, and then said that she herself was excited—riding on a train in the middle of the night, something she had never, in all her life, done before; and it didn't even matter that she didn't know where they were going; she couldn't wait to tell Paul; she wished he was there.

That's youth talking, Mrs. Walker thought. "It's like life's journey, it is," she said and smiled wryly. "You never know where it's going to take you," at which Sophie, Flora, and Mary all laughed, though Lucy did not; and Mrs. Walker herself only gave a sad smile.

But there was Sir John and Lady Needham, Prickett Ellis,

Miss Weld (seemingly floating, wearing muslin), Lord and Lady Lexham, Lady Lovejoy, Miss Alice—Clarissa greeted them all and checked them off the guest-list in her mind. And oh how she wished Stella Bowles would leave her side and go and talk with someone else; she knew Stella did not like her (for they were neighbours and yet they never saw one another except in passing, on the street, or, like this, at parties, and what else could it possibly mean but that Stella did not like her?). But where was Elizabeth? (Clarissa's eyes, scanning across feathered and beflowered hats, over top hats and bowlers and even a few balding heads, searched the crowd.) "There she is," Clarissa said now to Colonel and Mrs. Garrod, pointing out her daughter in the crowd. "There's our Elizabeth!"

"I'm studying to be a veterinarian," Elizabeth was saying, "at The Royal College of Veterinary Surgeons, in Liverpool," talking with Eleanor Gibson and Katherine Truelock (the latter, a girlhood friend of her mother's—one of the few Elizabeth actually liked), who had not yet found their way to Clarissa through the growing crowd of guests continuing to stream into the station.

And now Clarissa let the arrivals wash over her (all the while trying to keep up with her mental check-list): there was Hugh Whitbread, whom she'd known *for-ever,* without poor

Evelyn of course, but well scrubbed and polished as always (that was Hugh); and Mr. Bowley, and Mrs. Hilbery, and Lady Mary Maddox ("A new hat?" she asked: she simply *must* reveal where she got it), and Mr. Quin, and Ralph Lyon, then Mrs. Mount, who'd grown old since she had last seen her (though she wouldn't say that of course); had she been ill? And Celia and Herbert Ainsty (nearing only their twenty-fifth, Celia told her), and Professor Brierly (who would no doubt discuss Milton), and Mrs. Dakers....

But it was Richard Dalloway, nervously checking his watch again—9.50—who was the first to greet Sally Seton, now Lady Rosseter, along with her husband John (the owner of cotton mills, Clarissa had told him), who had just come dashing into the station, more or less at the last minute—running late as usual, Sally said—as the taxicab driver had picked them up at their hotel and then, for some unknown reason, deposited them in front of Pancras, and so rattled had they been—for they never came into London (the traffic was positively harrowing)—that they had not protested. (And the train *was* about to take off; it had just been announced: Track Four.) And so they embraced, he and Sally, and after saying she hoped they weren't too late, hoped they hadn't missed anything, Sally immediately resumed her teasing of him, as she always had, still calling him, these thirty-odd

years later, introducing him to her husband, first as "Wickham"—
and laughing (for Clarissa had mistaken him for a Wickham
when they'd first met), and then as "My name is Dalloway" (his
response to the mistake)—and laughing again, which he could
now take good-naturedly, though the joke *had* worn thin; and it
was rather a disappointment—that Sally should still be repeating
the same jokes these thirty-plus years later; that she had lost the
freshness which once made her so fetching. But John Rosseter, a
tall, bald, lumbering man who looked rather uncomfortable in
his ill-fitting, formal clothes (Richard thought), seemed a likable
sort (they shook hands)—someone who appeared and whose
manly handshake suggested that he might share an interest in the
outdoors; he would talk with him.

"Where is Clarissa?" Sally asked, dramatically putting her
hand up over her eyes and scouring the crowd, looking this way
and that, just as the captain of a sea-battled ship searches for
the much-anticipated shoreline.

Richard looked around, then laughed. "Where is Clarissa,
indeed!" For the crowd had swelled.

"All aboard, all aboard for North Yorkshire, North Yorkshire;
all aboard for North Yorkshire, Track Four. Track Four," it was
announced, and Richard, apologising, said he would have to leave
them now; that he must direct everyone to the first two cars.

And so the murmuring guests, only some of whom had heard the announced destination ("We are going to North Yorkshire tonight!" "*Such* a long distance! Why so far?" "We'll never sleep!") began moving towards the train and, slowly, very slowly—though not from reluctance on the part of most of them, began boarding, being greeted as they did so by Wilkins and Lucy who, along with Mrs. Walker and the three other servants had occupied the cars a few minutes early so as to try to arrange things in advance.

But Clarissa was certain that everyone she had invited had not yet arrived, she said to Nancy Blow as they embraced (and what a lovely fragrance; lavender, was it?); she hoped that all of them would make it there on time. Where, for example, was Sally? Sally Rosseter and her husband. Well, there was Millicent Bruton (who did not like her), blowing in and looking like some stiff, victorious general fresh off the battlefield, Clarissa thought (she could picture the golden epaulettes glittering atop Lady Bruton's shoulders in the sun) as they shook hands, which was always somewhat agonising for her given the determined firmness of Lady Bruton's grasp—it was as if she were gritting her teeth; but she knew Dick would be pleased, for there was the biography, which she knew he needed, particularly now that he had resigned from the House.

And there! There were some of the others she had invited but had not yet seen: Sasha Richardson, smoking a cigarette— lovely and ravishing in a silvery, grey gauze; and yet there was always something so sad and solitary about her too, Clarissa thought—she did not enjoy life; Mrs. Durrant and Clara, Sir Harry, Willie Titcomb, Jim Hutton (but she could not see whether he was wearing red socks; she must look again once they were on the train, and if he was she must remember to point them out to Sally, for *that* was something Sally would appreciate); and there came Lord Gayton and Ralph Johnson, and the Brunners (who relayed the message that—at the last minute Mr. and Mrs. Bromley, much to their regret—would be unable to attend, to which Clarissa responded that she hoped everything was all right?); and Miss O'Keefe (who reminded her of a sly cat), and, oh, there, at some distance, there was Sally! She called to her— "Sally! Sally!" But it was no use; her voice could not rise above the roar of the crowd. She supposed she would have to wait until they were on the train. (And, she thought now, looking down at the floor so as not to have to engage anyone, to have a brief moment to herself, she had not seen Dick or Elizabeth for quite some time, though she assumed Dick was at the train directing people; and Elizabeth had been in good hands when last she had seen her, talking with dear Katherine Truelock and her Eleanor.)

Oh, but there were more, more of her guests, all of whom she saw now only at a distance—Lily Everit, Bob Brinsley, her beloved Mrs. Vallance, dignified in black lace (holding an ornate, silver-headed walking-stick); and Jack Renshaw, Roderick Serle and Ruth Anning (dressed in purple velvet); Mira Cartwright, Mabel Waring, Ellen Barnet (on crutches, poor thing), Rose Shaw (who, Clarissa thought, looked cheap), Charles Burt, Mrs. Holman, Bertram Pritchard, and there, lastly, she thought, Miss Milan and Robert Haydon, running for the train (oh, there went her hat! She would have to stop and retrieve it. She did). Miss Milan and Robert Haydon running hand in hand (a new couple? Clarissa wondered now).

AND SO, AT 10 P.M. (give or take a minute or two), the train began to move; or rather (so Robert Davies observed, for he had somehow managed to blend in with the crowd and sneak onto the train unnoticed), it was that by-now old and familiar (if unsettling) sensation of the train standing still and the station itself beginning to pull away, particularly if one were seated backwards, facing *away* from the direction in which the train was moving, as he was now, at the back of the last of the two Dalloway cars, one car and the length of another from Richard and his wife.

"Such crowded quarters!" Mrs. Walker laughed good-naturedly as the train jerked forward. "I'm all elbows," she crowed, still laughing and trying to maneuver—along with Lucy, Sophie, Mary, and Flora—behind the makeshift table that had been set-up at the head of the second car so that it might be situated between the two. "And such noise, too."

And there was a din, Clarissa noticed, while Lady Bruton addressed her, as usual, on some topic of interest to Lady Bruton but of none whatsoever to her—in this case Lady Bruton's obsession with what she saw as the poor character of the French people (with which Clarissa disagreed); there was a din, that constant buzz or hum of conversation which always signalled that a party was going well. But it was early, she reminded herself, it was early, and there was the novelty of the party being on a train: she must stay on her guard. And as she looked about, noticing that some people were sitting, some standing, suddenly, above all the noise she heard her husband's voice; he was asking everyone to please open their windows, for between the sweet, pungent smell of the flowers and the crowded cars, he said....

There is Richard (Lady Bruton thought), asking people to open windows. And it *was* stuffy in there; otherwise, she supposed, they might all suffocate (and here a picture briefly formed in her mind of the train arriving at its destination, the doors being opened and all of the passengers on those two cars being found dead on the floor, like so many soldiers in the trenches of a battlefield). But she must seek out Richard—they had not yet seen one another; they would talk; for, looking through her family papers one evening last week, to which there had recently been fresh additions, she had discovered something new and astonishing about her uncle, Sir General Talbot Moore, something which—she knew—Richard would be interested to hear. She liked Richard Dalloway, she found him admirable; he had a certain—what was it?—a certain *something* (for she was not good with words). What a relief it would be, too, talking with him after spending time with Clarissa, which was like talking to—what? To thin air. It had always been like that; it was a feeling of immateriality; of insubstantiality, as if—whatever one's thoughts and opinions were on this or that, whatever one had to say, was unimportant; made no difference whatsoever; floated off and vanished. No, Lady Bruton thought, she did not understand such marriages as Richard and Clarissa Dalloway's. (Should Richard, therefore, be regarded as less admirable because of it? she asked herself. Now *there* was a question for the philosophers.) And to have lasted thirty years! Well, she was certainly glad that *she* had not married.

But wasn't that that Mr. Faber who had visited Father this

afternoon? Elizabeth Dalloway asked herself as the train began to pick up speed leaving the station. She had observed the man dressed all in white (save for a silly, rather sad, and soiled-looking green carnation) and slumped down in the last seat, glistening with perspiration. Yes, she thought so. And then she had a most amusing thought—that because his face was gleaming and his white tuxedo so shiny, he looked rather like the mercury in a thermometer of someone with a very high fever. (Will he gauge the temperature of the party? she wondered). And, she continued, trying to amuse and distract herself (for she would much prefer to be alone in the country), he looked, too, like the White Rabbit in Lewis Carroll's book. But she would have to find Katherine Truelock and her friend again, Miss What'shername?, Elizabeth resolved (playing with her long hair), for they had been fun to talk with. Or *interesting*, as the adults would say. She looked back and into the crowded car now only to see Lady Hosford slowly edging towards her—like a burrowing mole (Elizabeth thought). Or a snail. And in response, she spun around quickly and approached Mr. Faber; she said hello, re-introduced herself, and then tried to appear engaged with him (as Lady Hosford neared) as she asked if he remembered meeting her that afternoon.

"Yes, of course I remember you," Robbie said, sitting up in his seat, running one hand through his hair and hoping that he appeared—at least relatively—sober. "Yes, how are you?" he went on (for he was grateful for the company). "Elizabeth, isn't it? Awfully hot in here..." (and all the while thinking that this Elizabeth must look like her mother, for she did not look at all like Richard).

And Elizabeth said that yes, it *was* hot, and that she would much prefer to be out there (she gestured towards the window), where she was sure it must be cool.

"Yes, and it *has* stopped raining," Robbie said, fanning himself with his hand, glancing out the window and noting that he felt rather sorry for the poor girl, for she seemed quite out of place; uncomfortable. Like him (he thought now). And so he would go along with her; he would make small talk. But then he could think of nothing further to say and nor, it seemed, could she. And so, just as both of them earlier that afternoon had turned their gaze up the stairway in anticipation of Richard Dalloway's descent, Robert Davies and Elizabeth Dalloway now turned and looked into the crowd of party-goers, seeking—once again—some interruption, some relief from this terrible awkwardness.

But she was in Florence in May, the grey and misty vision that was Sasha Richardson said to Clarissa Dalloway, responding to the question of why on earth she had not attended the Chelsea Flower Show last month, which Clarissa told her had been "splendid!"—a big improvement over the previous year's show (which, in all fairness, had been hurt by the bad winter they'd had).

In Florence with her father (Sasha Richardson added); he had been there on business. And so she was left to herself most days; free to roam the city (she blew perfect smoke-rings out into the car). She had walked endlessly, she said (rather blandly, Clarissa thought; rather listlessly)—along the Arno; across the Ponte de Vecchio; into the Uffizi Gallery....

How lovely for her! Clarissa said enthusiastically, for she wanted in the worst way to cheer, to save, this poor lost soul; for life was valuable, and all-too brief, and Sasha Richardson, all of what—twenty-three?—must be taught that, she must know it in her heart.

But the last time *she* had been on the continent—Sasha was fortunate to have gone so recently, Clarissa continued—was the previous year when she and Richard had taken Elizabeth on her first trip to Paris (which Elizabeth had of course loved). Oh, but yes, she too adored Florence, she assured Sasha Richardson now; *adored* it; she thought the city itself a work of art; in fact, she went on, hearing about Sasha's experiences made her think that she and Richard should return to Florence soon, for they had not been there in—what was it?—could it really be?—1907, twenty years. She imagined that the city had changed considerably in twenty years, as so much of the world had changed since the War; yes, perhaps she and Richard should go to Florence on a second honeymoon.

But Clarissa could see over Sasha Richardson's shoulder that the servants finally had what Mrs. Walker was calling their "station" set up. Would Sasha like anything? A watercress sandwich? A cake? No? A glass of wine, then? Or a cup of tea?

Should they wait for everyone to come to them, Lucy wondered aloud, or should she and Wilkins try to walk through the cars carrying the trays? Yes, she thought the latter, she said— otherwise, such a crowd would gather and step over themselves and scarcely be able to move, and it would be impossible.

And Mrs. Walker, overhearing Lucy, paused amidst the song she was whistling (it was "My Wild Irish Rose," wasn't it? someone in the crowd asked), Mrs. Walker said that yes, she agreed, that she, too, thought it a good idea (for it would take some of the work off her so that she might poke her head out the window and sneak a fag).

But Wilkins was not for it, he said. For he (a compulsive worrier) was convinced that just as he and Lucy were to fill and pick up a tray, the train would jolt and rock, and then they would pitch forwards or sideways or—worse—backwards and spill the food and the wine all over the guests. And then where would they be?

"And aren't the flowers lovely?" Clarissa said to everyone in her general area within hearing distance, hoping to distract them from the servants' bickering, spreading her arms as if to encircle and take them all in. "Dick bought them for me this morning."

Following the voice she had heard saying something about the flowers, "Clarissa's voice," Sally Rosseter told her husband (for she would know it anywhere; it was like—what?—like bells!), she made her way through the crowd. (But it was just like Richard, Sally thought, now digesting what Clarissa had said, it was just like Richard to buy the flowers. For there had always been something—was "feminine" the right word? There had always been that *something*, whatever it was, about him, in spite of his love of the outdoors: it was something soft; something pliant and unmanly. For she couldn't imagine her John buying the flowers; not for the life of her. *Or* giving a party for that matter.) But there! There was Clarissa! "Clarissa!" she called out. And Clarissa Dalloway beamed (*and* brightened, Sally thought) and walked over to her. And they embraced, spilled into each other's arms, both colouring and awkwardly pouring forth a stream of words (behind each other's ear, as they embraced) which neither of them caught.

"How marvelous you look," Sally said now, holding Clarissa's arms and stepping away from her. "Doesn't Clarissa look marvelous, John?" she asked (reaching for her husband so as to introduce him and draw him into the conversation).

My, he is shy, Clarissa thought, shaking John Rosseter's hand. This big, handsome, block of a man is shy (she was touched). She still couldn't get over how much the worse for wear Sally looked—all the vitality and lustre that had made her so irresistible to everyone at Bourton (or almost everyone, she recalled, thinking of Aunt Helena), all that now seemingly gone. She'd grown even fatter (since the last time she had seen her), and grey, and Bourton was the past—what was there to say?

"How are your boys?" she asked, which was a mistake. For off Sally went, her sails puffed—how this one was at Oxford; that one in China working as a missionary, and this one here and that one there and, oh, her youngest, Rupert.... "And Elizabeth?" Sally finally asked when she had come to the end of her maternal rhapsody: "How is Elizabeth?"

"Elizabeth is quite well," Clarissa answered, detecting a note of falseness, or condescension, in Sally's voice. Or was it competitiveness? Or superiority? "She's here somewhere," Clarissa laughed, gesturing out towards the two cars. (But it enraged her, this "How's Elizabeth?" of Sally's at the end of her litany about her five boys, as if Elizabeth, being only one—and a girl—was...what? Somehow less. And from Sally of all people!)

"She's studying to be a veterinarian at the Royal School in Liverpool," Clarissa dropped as modestly but as deftly as she could into Sally's lap, immediately noticing that her words had had the desired effect, as Sally's eyes widened—she was surprised. And impressed. Oh, but she hated this competing coming between them; it was so silly. She must seek common ground. And then she had it. "Peter Walsh sent a wire," she told Sally. "Peter wired us from India to offer his congratulations."

"Peter!" Sally said, turning to her husband, still trying to bring him into the conversation. "I've told you about Peter Walsh, John. At Bourton."

John Rosseter nodded.

"Do you hear from him?" Clarissa asked.

Sally rolled her eyes (that was the old Sally!). "About once a year only," she said. "Dull, dull, dull—always about how he and Daisy and her two children did this or that."

Yes, Clarissa agreed (thinking that love, especially new love, does make one seem dull to others); yes, his letters *were* dull sticks. But what fun they'd had at Bourton. And so back in time they went, back to Bourton, as John Rosseter and the crowd around them seemed to vanish, to veer out of focus and into the background while Bourton came to the fore. "Joseph Breitkopf's singing Brahms so miserably" (Sally laughed); "and remember the plans we made" (Clarissa said), "talking in my bedroom until all hours of the night—how we were going to abolish private property? Absurd, wasn't it? And reading Plato and Shelley?" Sally asked if Clarissa remembered how Peter Walsh and old Hugh Whitbread—Hugh was old even then, though he was but our age—if she remembered how Peter and Hugh hadn't got on because Hugh was always dropping everything for his "dear mother," as he called her? If Hugh had plans on a particular day but his mum wanted him to take her to Bath on that very same day, said Sally, his plans would go to hell and he would take her to Bath. "How that enraged Peter," Sally laughed.

"All those summer nights," Clarissa went on, saying that not only had Peter not liked Hugh, but he hadn't liked Dick either (and, Sally thought, neither had she; while Clarissa thought the very same thing, remembering her rage when Sally had said that Dick would never be in the Cabinet because he had a second-class brain). But Peter eventually came around, Clarissa said. And there is Dick now, she observed, having spotted the top of his head in the crowd. So she and Sally remembered; so they laughed; and so the old feelings began to come back to them.

But Lady Hosford had snared Elizabeth and was asking her who on earth that ridiculous and rather disheveled and, she must say, *inappropriate*-looking man was—the one dressed all in white she had seen Elizabeth talking to (thinking him some friend of Elizabeth's but not, she hoped, a boyfriend). To which Elizabeth responded, telling Lady Hosford all she knew, that it was a Mr. Frank Faber, a friend of her father's—that he had been at the house that very afternoon. She tried, without being rude, to move on (for she *had* something of great import to tell her father, she said), feeling relieved that Lady Hosford had—at least—not asked any of the by now all-too-familiar questions, nor had she corrected Elizabeth in any way nor said any of the things that she usually said.

And all the while Robert Davies continued to sit alone in the last seat of the train car, facing backwards, occasionally having to retreat into the next car (with yet another group of rather startled looking strangers) when Richard grew too close, talking to no one, and no one talking to him. What's wrong with me? he asked himself. Why isn't anyone talking to me? (He turned sideways so as to look down the car. Well, there was the wine coming his way.) It was as if he were invisible (was he?). Was it what Bob Willoughby called "the Wilde syndrome"? Or was it simply that none of them knew him, as they seemed to know one another—all of them having attended other parties at the Dalloways' home no doubt (and here he pictured what he had seen of the house). So he resolved to make an effort. He would stand up; he would approach people; he would introduce himself. But *how* would he introduce himself; or rather, as *whom*? Could he be himself, Robert Davies, or should he be Frank Faber? Frank Faber, he thought now, a friend of Richard's, he would say. No, no relation to the publisher, though he did work there—as an editor; and yes, it was an odd coincidence, wasn't it?—but that was life. Yes, he would mingle; he would work his way through the crowd (for he wanted to see what Richard's wife looked like); he would walk through both cars until—there, there he stood, before Richard. And then he would say what? "Hello." For that was all he could say, unless he wanted to blow it all to hell. Or, he thought (standing up), perhaps it would be better if he waited, if he avoided Richard at all cost, until they got to wherever it was they were going (assuming that they were going *somewhere*) and disembarked from the train, for then there would be more space, more room, potentially, for privacy, so that he would not embarrass Richard. But what *was* this party? Where *was* Richard going? Running away from him?

Hadn't Mrs. Vallance looked at him somewhat askance? Richard Dalloway asked himself, looking out the train window (it had stopped raining) so as to momentarily avoid the guests. Yes, he thought that she had—looked at him rather oddly, disapprovingly, meaning to slight him—her old, yellow eyes narrowing; her cracked, reddened lips pursed in disgust. Did she know—was that possible? Could she, somehow, have found out? Or had Clarissa told her? (No, Clarissa would not do that; would not tell her—nor anyone.) But how glad he was now, he realised, that he and Clarissa had at the last minute decided against inviting Dr. Blitzer, for he could just picture Blitzer, with his sharp, pointed little beard, standing across the room—his arms folded over his chest—scrutinising him through his spectacles (or so it would have felt). And of course there had been that fiasco with Bradshaw at the previous party; but oh, he was tired, he thought, as the landscape out the window seemed to rush past him (plunging through the midlands as they were), flashing in the summer twilight—tree, house, field, cow.... It was as his day had been; a rush of images, happenings—walking through the park; the brothers on the bench; flowers at Mulberry's; books at Hatchards'; going to Robbie's (and indeed, his recalling all of the difficulties with Robbie, and Clarissa understanding); and Duncan's visit, and so many memories, including—no, he could not think of that. And stepping back from the window now, instead of seeing whatever it was that the train was passing at that very instant, Richard Dalloway saw his own reflection. It was a sobering sight. For it served to remind him (so he interpreted it) that he *must* stay alert; *must* remember the party (life was a series of such commands); it was for Clarissa after all, and whether Mrs. Vallance or anyone else knew about him or not, he should not be thinking of himself; he had responsibilities—the party was his gift to Clarissa (and she deserved it; for she understood), and he would, he *must,* make it shine for her.

Someone had pinched her on the arse! Lucy whispered to Mrs. Walker, her eyes popping.

"Who?" Mrs. Walker demanded, her hair falling down in ringlets about her face, which was now aflame with colour. She and Lucy looked out into the crowd of guests.

But Lucy said she did not know: she had been standing over there (she pointed); there, where, standing now, Wilkins was serving people they all knew from previous parties—that poor (beautiful) Miss Richardson, Mr. and Mrs. Brunner, and Lord Gayton—none of whom, she was sure, would do such a thing.

Well, Mrs. Walker insisted, still red-faced, they would have to tell the master, that was all there was to it. For they could not.... But Lucy interrupted her; saying no (and putting her hands on her hips), that they mustn't tell anyone, for she would not spoil the party. It had happened to *her,* she said, and she forbade Mrs. Walker to tell Mr. Dalloway or anyone else about it.

"What's all this whispering?" Sophie asked now, swooping down on them like a crane, and so Mrs. Walker told her and the other girls what had happened, pointing in the same direction that Lucy had just pointed.

"Maybe it was Wilkins!" Sophie suggested, an idea which all five of them found so ludicrous that they burst out laughing.

"Sussex," Katherine Truelock exclaimed in response to Elizabeth Dalloway's mention of the place she wanted to live. "Eleanor and I live in Sussex. Near Firle. We've been trying for years to get your mother to come out for a visit. The both of you should come."

Elizabeth said she would like that; she would like it very much—perhaps some time that summer, if it was all right?

"July, August." Eleanor Gibson said. "Anytime. We'll be around all summer" (and here she looked at Katherine)—"heeding the call of a rather demanding garden; we would love to see you both."

And so Elizabeth asked Eleanor to tell her all about where she and Katherine lived and what it was like—for as Katherine probably knew, she said, she had grown up in dreary old London.

While Eleanor was answering Elizabeth's question, saying that she and Katherine lived in a lovely old eighteenth-century stone farmhouse, surrounded by downs and the river Ouse, and what a difference having a motor car made now, Katherine was looking at Elizabeth and thinking how surprised she was—that she never would have guessed that a daughter of Clarissa Dalloway's could end up like this; she felt proud of both of them.

Two women, their age, living together, Elizabeth mused, saying aloud how lovely their house sounded. Should she mention Miss Kilman? she wondered now, for it seemed possible that they might have known her (though she doubted it). But yes, she would have a farm in Sussex, she told them instead; a farm, where she would run her practice and have animals of her own—a horse (or two), and milking cows, and dogs and cats, and other farm animals.

"I always wished I had a daughter," Sally said to Clarissa, each holding a glass of wine as they looked at Elizabeth from afar (she's handsome, thought Clarissa); (horsy, and still awkward, Sally thought, thinking, too, that she and John could have done better). "But we tried," Sally laughed, shrugging. "I was thirty-eight when Rupert, our youngest, was born, and Dr. Lawrence strongly advised that we stop after him."

"And Dick always wished we had had a boy or two," Clarissa added.

And Sally could just imagine how *he* would have turned out, she thought—this Richard Dalloway, Jr.

"But I feel as though I'm a mother to so many young people nowadays," Clarissa went on, "that I'm perfectly happy." Ah! And there were two of her "children" now, Clarissa said, pointing out Mira Cartwright and Sasha Richardson as they made their way through the car, arm-in-arm. She knew that Sally would fall in love with Sasha, as most people did.

"But tell me, Clarissa," Sally asked now, "do you know where it is that we are going?"

Clarissa laughed and shook her head. "No," she said, then went on laughing.

And Sally laughed too; for it *was* funny—two train cars full of, what?—some fifty or sixty people, shuttling through the midlands in the middle of the night, and perhaps only one of them knew where in the world they were going.

"But what was it you used to say at Bourton?" Clarissa asked Sally. "Something about it being not the destination but the journey that mattered most?"

To which Sally waved her hand dismissively, as if to indicate that *that* was then and this was now.

And that was it, Clarissa mused: that was what was wrong; it was as if Sally were repudiating her former self.

But she was sure John would know where they were going, Sally thought—that either Richard would have told him, for she had seen them, out of the corner of her eye, talking together, or that he would have figured it out for himself. She would ask him.

And just past Sally, Clarissa could see the Brunners, standing there talking only to one another, as they always did at her parties; talking and eating their sandwiches. It was either that or standing together and not talking. My, but they are dull, she thought. (But now Lady Hosford stepped into her circle, embraced Sally and immediately lit into some story about Bourton.) Should she make an effort to include the Brunners, Clarissa wondered, to try to bring them into the party (as she always did)? Or should she just resolve not to invite them again?

"Now I'm focussing all of my considerable scholarly skills on Matthew Arnold," Professor Brierly professed to the man who had just introduced himself as Frank Faber.

But wasn't that quite a jump? Robert Davies asked this professor, historically speaking—from Milton to Arnold, certain that he could, if he chose to, sustain this conversation through the entire night by merely inserting a comment here and a question there (for this fellow is full of himself, Robbie thought, smiling as Brierly began carefully constructing his defense).

"Do you know where it is that we are going?" Eleanor Gibson—her back to Lady Hosford—asked Elizabeth Dalloway, looking at Katherine Truelock all the while.

"No," Elizabeth answered, shaking her head. "Father has

kept it a secret. Even from me," she smiled, hoping Lady
Hosford would not turn around.

And Katherine said that she and Eleanor were certain *they*
knew, and furthermore that they would tell her if she liked. "But
you must promise to keep it a secret as long as your father does."
Elizabeth smiled again and nodded, and the three women leaned
close together as Katherine whispered into Elizabeth's ear.

And there were Claire Milan and Robert Haydon (Clarissa
observed, as Lady Hosford and Sally went on and on). They were
standing in the same place they had stood since the train left
King's Cross; holding hands; looking starry-eyed. I was right, she
thought—they *are* in love. Perhaps they would announce their
engagement that very night, on her and Dick's anniversary.

"But really, you must come visit us some time when we're at
Fellstree," Richard Dalloway was saying to John Rosseter. "You
and Sally." For, just as he had suspected, this Rosseter was a
fellow after his own heart; a true countryman; he had grown up
in Shropshire.

"I'd like that," Rosseter replied. "And you must join our
annual fox-hunt in late September." He was relaxing; becoming
expansive. "Manchester is spectacular at that time of the year.
And the boys usually all try to come along if they can, from
wherever they are at the time. One—Gordon—is in China of all

places," he added, referring to his sons. "All except Rupert that is. The youngest," he added. "We make a weekend of it," he brightened. "Sally cooks, and...."

"Well then I think I *shall* join you," Richard interjected enthusiastically, thinking *why not?*—now that he had the time; why shouldn't he join them? But he and Clarissa and possibly Elizabeth, he told John Rosseter (by the way, did he know, had Sally told him, that Elizabeth was in veterinary school? "Indeed, she is. At the Royal College in Liverpool"), he and Clarissa and possibly Elizabeth were planning to spend all of August and the first week of September at Fellstree, and anytime he and Sally and any or all of their boys liked, or just himself alone, if Sally and the boys couldn't come; anytime he could visit would be fine (and he was sure it would be fine with Clarissa too, he told himself). They could hunt wild game, he went on; they could fish; they could go punting in the river—"Sally and Clarissa could join us for that, if they liked."

"Weren't they, Clarissa?" Sally asked her. But Clarissa Dalloway had not been listening.

"Weren't they what?" she answered, telling Sally that she hadn't heard her over the crowd.

"Lady Hosford and I were just saying how splendid those summers at Bourton were."

"Of another era," Lady Hosford added wistfully; she had been born shortly after Queen Victoria took the throne.

"Oh my, yes," Clarissa Dalloway said now, thinking that it was those summers at Bourton which had spun her off into adult life; for it was there that she had met Sally, Peter Walsh, and most importantly, she supposed, Richard. (But it was there, too, she thought silently, that she had stood alone at the windows; waiting.)

"Ah, love, let us be true to one another…" Lady Bruton now overheard someone say. But who was speaking? The voice was familiar; she was certain she had heard it somewhere before. She turned around and saw, there, backed into a corner—it was that professor, Professor What'shisname? He taught at, oh, where was it?—not Oxford or Cambridge; not one of the big schools. She had met him at another of Richard's parties; literature was his field; she remembered that; he had a specialty he was always spouting off about—some obscure writer. It was him, that professor, speaking to another man, someone she did not know, tall and thin and dressed all in white. But had she heard right? Had the professor actually addressed this fellow as "love," right there in front of everyone? Well, of course she knew such a thing existed, but not that *she* herself had ever witnessed, certainly not in her family, not in the military, and not at one of Richard Dalloway's parties either! Really, the nerve of some people (she thought). I, for one, am offended; and I am sure I am not alone. They should be thrown off the train! Where was Richard? She would tell him at once.

"And we are here as on a darkling plain/Swept with confused alarms of struggle and flight,/Where ignorant armies clash by night."

Robert Davies applauded softly so as not to call attention to himself (but to appease Brierly), for he could now see Richard (with his back to him), standing at the head of the car.

Oh, he is merely reciting a poem, Lady Bruton thought, feeling relieved. But she needn't feel embarrassed, she told herself (though she did), for she had merely been on her guard, as one should be. And what was it the professor had said? Something about armies clashing, wasn't that it? She would have to ask him about the poem and tell him about her uncle.

But then there was a bell; or rather a bell-like sound, a constant ringing—("a pinging," Lucy described it); ("a tinkling," Lady Hosford thought)—as Wilkins gently hit two crystal glasses together again and again and, when the crowd had finally quieted, said that his master had an announcement to make.

And now for the first time since the train had left King's

Cross Station, for a brief second or two, only the clacking sounds of the train rushing along the tracks were audible.

So Richard Dalloway stood up on a seat, in the hopes of looking both ways and seeing *all* of his guests in *that* car (for he had already made the announcement in the other car); he ducked his head and held onto the side of the car so as to maintain his balance, while the train hurtled on.

(And Robbie, seeing Richard suddenly standing atop the seat, quickly excused himself and retreated into the next car so that he would not be found out. Ah, but seeing Richard, standing there, Richard's body, Robbie could not help but think about how their bodies were a perfect fit—even Richard said so; for that *was* part of it, part of what was between them.)

("He is going to tell us!" someone in the crowd whispered.)

(There is Richard, Lady Bruton thought; the dignified statesman. He had an announcement—standing there, she presumed, just as, time and time again, he had stood on the floor of the House.)

"For those of you who don't already know," Richard Dalloway said, checking his watch—it was 1.30—"we are on our way to North Yorkshire" (he paused and took a breath, giving the moment the full, dramatic effect that it deserved). "We are one of thirty-six trains which are being run from London to view, weather permitting, the total eclipse of the sun!"

There was a collective gasp from the fifty or sixty guests in the two cars. This was followed by a kind of awed silence, as if to honor the ingenuity of their host; and finally a gentle murmur of conversation resumed and there were smiles all around.

"Some fifteen thousand of us are expected from London alone," Richard continued (far more verbose than he had been in his announcement in the first car, perhaps as a result of Clarissa's presence?). "A total eclipse of the sun has not been visible in Britain for fifty years! And at North Yorkshire we will be in what they call 'the totality belt'" (he paused and looked at Clarissa, who held her hands over her heart and looked back at him admiringly). "Which simply means *that* is where the totality of the eclipse will be most fully visible."

(Here Hugh Whitbread consulted his clippings from that morning's *Times,* finding the map depicting this belt of totality. He ran his finger over the page: it ranged, he noted, from around Sunderland in the north, to Saltburn in the south.)

Again the crowd seemed to take in air, to momentarily hold its breath and release it. And then they applauded him (and he bowed). And slowly, as the applause died out and Richard Dalloway stepped down from the seat on which he had been standing and proceeded in the direction of his wife, conversation once again resumed.

"I was right!" Hugh Whitbread said proudly to Sasha Richardson, whom he had known since she was a baby. Nothing gets by me (he thought, fingering his lapels and taking a bite out of yet another ham sandwich). What Evelyn was missing, he exclaimed to Sasha (who, finding him a bore but being too polite to show it, nodded graciously and lit another cigarette), thinking, too, that Evelyn missed sharing so many of life's experiences with him; he might as well live alone.

And Elizabeth Dalloway smiled at Katherine Truelock and Eleanor Gibson: the secret they had shared with her was now out; and she was so proud of her father.

"And *we will be* on a darkling plain," Professor Brierly said with a smirk, modifying Matthew Arnold in response to Richard Dalloway's announcement. He was speaking, once again, to Robert Davies, who had re-entered the car as soon as he'd seen Richard stand down (for he had found it somewhat humiliating, humiliating and perhaps all-too symbolic, standing in the next car and peering through the window, and he had wanted to put an end to it as quickly as possible).

But what was it Richard had said? Robbie wondered now. Perhaps...(he thought). No. But he could think it; hope it—

that Richard had renounced his marriage and proclaimed his love for *him*. But he knew that Richard had most likely announced their destination. He would have to ask this Brierly fellow, *if* he could get a word in. For there was something terribly unnerving to him about this speeding through the darkness and not knowing where one was going. It was a feeling he had experienced many times in his life, the absurd feeling that he was hurrying nowhere fast—and all the while the bell clocks were ringing off the time. At such moments his heart raced and his pulse seemingly pumped volumes of blood through his veins in a very short time, and all the while his breathing sounded like so many horses cantering across an open field. And to what end? For what purpose? He did not know if he should slow down, or reverse direction. It seemed a pointless, too rapid journey with no destination, the mere thought of which was terrifying.

"What a marvelous idea!" Clarissa Dalloway said, now embracing her husband, standing—as she had been during his announcement—with Sally Rosseter and Lady Hosford. To blend their thirtieth wedding anniversary, she said, not only to Richard but to everyone within hearing distance (pearl, was it? she knew that the fiftieth was gold), to blend their anniversary and the other important event of the day—a total eclipse of the sun. It was an idea, she said, she was convinced only her Dick could have come up with.

Again there was a small round of applause. And John Rosseter, standing behind his wife, extended his hand to Richard Dalloway, congratulating him on what he proclaimed "a splendid idea."

Whereupon Lady Bruton said that she, too, found it admirable; heroic, even.

And Richard Dalloway, blushing, did feel proud.

Then Sally took over and immediately began to tease him, saying how surprised she was—that this was the sort of grand gesture which seemed more characteristic of Wickham than "'My name is Dalloway.'"

But her joke fell flat. John Rosseter, clearly embarrassed, looked away; Richard and Clarissa exchanged the quick, sympathetically expressive glances of two people whose lives were irrevocably intertwined.

But then Sally, trying to recover, raised her glass and—in a loud voice—announced a toast: "To the Dalloways!"

"To the Dalloways!" the guests echoed, as the ring of their glasses touching resounded throughout the two cars.

And Lady Hosford, still puzzled by Sally's attempted jokes, said, "Thirty years."

"Yes," Clarissa said, looking into her husband's eyes. "How time has flown; it seems more like three...."

"And here's to thirty more!" Hugh Whitbread called out, and again the glasses rang.

He was beside himself, Wilkins said to Lucy and Mrs. Walker; beside himself with joy. For he had been reading all about this eclipse in the papers, and now he would witness it for himself, first-hand. It was something to tell his cronies about, it was.

And Mrs. Walker exclaimed that it might be something of a miracle but it still wouldn't bring her dear Joe back; and Lucy said she only wished that Paul was there to see it with her.

She and Eleanor had been excited about this day, the eclipse, for weeks and weeks, Katherine Truelock told Elizabeth now. They had been so proud to read in that morning's *Times* that an American woman—her name was Caroline Furness, Katherine said she believed—an American woman who directed the observatory at Vassar College in New York, this Caroline Furness, *a woman,* was travelling over to watch what was called the "flash spectrum."

(But superimposing itself and taking precedence over her curiosity about what the "flash spectrum" might be was Elizabeth's question to herself as to whether or not *now* was the time to introduce Miss Kilman's name into the conversation.)

Having made his announcement and received Clarissa's (and the crowd's) approval, Richard Dalloway found his way over to the servants' table and sat down by it for a moment to rest, hoping to avoid, at least briefly, all conversation. For he wanted time, time to revel in his achievement, yes, but also, time to ponder this question of how people changed over the years; he was thinking specifically of Sally Seton. (It amazed him how— with all of the experience he had garnered during his years in the House—he felt as though he knew very little about the human character, for he had not studied it.) But this matter of how people—Sally—changed. It was as if Sally Seton (those thirty-some years ago at Bourton) and Lady Rosseter (now) were two completely separate and different people. They *looked* different, he thought—Sally Seton had shone, had been dark and beautiful; whereas Lady Rosseter was dull, grey, and matronly. (But was this simply age, and was he being unfair?) He thought not, because the two Sallys acted so differently as well. Where Sally Seton was passionate and daring, Lady Rosseter seemed stale and staid; and there was no trace whatsoever of the former Sally, or none that he could see. And then (now looking out the window into the dark night), he remembered one of the questions he had asked himself that very afternoon—if Duncan would have stayed the same had he lived. He supposed he had to admit that if such a dramatic change could happen to Sally, then it could happen to anyone, that it was possible. He would ask Clarissa's opinion, for it was a character question, about which she was an expert. (And it also occurred to him now that perhaps it had been wrong of him, wrong-headed certainly, and possibly even immoral, to still be clinging to Duncan like he was, and to have allowed Duncan's death, perhaps unconsciously, to cast such a long shadow over his own life.)

But Clarissa hasn't much changed since Bourton, he thought (upon hearing her voice); which caused him to wonder *which* Sally John Rosseter had married, and if he had been, over time, disappointed? Nor have *I* changed much—at least not that I recognise, he reasoned. But then the thought occurred to him that perhaps Sally was standing over there (he looked in her direction, she was still talking with Clarissa and Lady Hosford), perhaps she was standing there and thinking the very same things about him.

And there, now, more immediately, was Mrs. Walker directly in front of him, waving her finger and saying that she had a bone to pick with someone, with whom she wasn't quite sure—should she speak with him?—it was his party after all—or Mrs. Dalloway?—for really, she was the one who ran everything—or Lady Hosford? Or should she go directly to the offending party herself, that Miss Atkins. For she was quite put out, Mrs. Walker told him now (again red in the face), having to stand there all night working her fingers to the bone while this Miss Atkins, this *servant* ("for that's what she is, sir") dressed in street clothes, went around drinking wine and eating—eating food *she* had made, and talking with the guests and putting on airs "as if she were one of them!" Mrs. Walker said that it was the same as if she, herself, were to take off her apron right then and there and walk into the crowd. And how would he like that? It was not right, she said. Not fair to herself, to Lucy and Wilkins, nor to the three specially hired girls.

Yes, I see, Mr. Dalloway said to Mrs. Walker, saying, too, that he understood. But this *is* a bind, he thought, remembering how—not long ago—Clarissa had commented that the role of servants had changed considerably since the War. And she had been right. But this was a matter he *could* handle, he resolved; one with which he had a good deal of experience—diplomacy; compromise. He would—what? He would talk to Lady Hosford. Surely she would understand and then deal with Miss Atkins herself, directly.

"I'll have it in hand momentarily," he said to Mrs. Walker, who smiled and thanked him.

But should he speak with Clarissa about it first? he

wondered, looking in the direction where his wife had stood with Sally and Lady Hosford just moments ago. But she was no longer there. Where was she? His eyes searched the crowd until, there, standing by an open window, he saw her—a shimmering, white silhouette. She, too, he thought, needed a moment to herself; he would not interrupt her. He would go directly to Lady Hosford.

Clarissa had had to withdraw for a moment, which, she felt, was awkward—for there was nowhere to go, really, no place to hide, no "other room" as she had at home (and there she was, once again, standing at an open window). Awkward, yes, but she hoped it was not rude; for she needed a brief respite, because—because Sally had mentioned Aunt Helena. Aunt Helena, she thought, sighing, breathing in the night air and exhaling a fathomless longing that had stayed with her throughout her life; Aunt Helena, who—well into her eighties—had always come into town for their parties; she hadn't missed a one. She had been at the last party they'd had, in Westminster, obviously failing; she had no sooner been placed in a chair when she fell asleep, poor thing, but she had come; and then she had died—the previous September. (Yes, she thought, Big Ben beat on and on, sparing no one.)

And she *had* had a rather miserable life, Clarissa supposed;

had seemingly turned bitter early on. Was it losing her mother, her sister-in-law, and best friend, so young? Clarissa wondered, as she herself had lost Sylvia. And then she immediately thought how odd it was that people reacted to similar situations so differently. But then each of us *is* different (she went on thinking), which was one of the things that made something like this (she looked around)—a party—so fascinating (if it worked). But how Aunt Helena, in her white Cashmere shawl at Bourton, always going on about her book on the orchids of Burma and how it went into three editions before 1870, how Aunt Helena had taken a dislike to Sally (she thought, now looking over in Sally's direction and thinking she should be getting back)—it was as if Aunt Helena, for reasons known only to her (or perhaps unknown), it was as if she were taking out all of her bitter feelings on Sally.

"Most astronomers are interested in the corona," Hugh Whitbread, having put on his spectacles, now read aloud. It was a clipping from that morning's *Times* which he had brought along—folded up in his coat pocket. Professor Brierly nodded and brushed a few crumbs from Hugh Whitbread's lapels, who then, though slightly taken aback by this impertinence on the professor's part, continued. "And in consequence they must take up their stations on the central line of totality or as near to it as possible." (And here Hugh Whitbread looked up at

Professor Brierly to make sure that he still had his attention, which he did, and then he traced his finger along the page and mumbled to himself to indicate that he was skimming, searching, for—there it was.

"Here it is," he said to Brierly. "Here is the exercise I told you about. 'Pass a half-crown centrally over a florin,'" Hugh Whitbread read instructionally, and the professor dutifully reached into his trouser pocket, pulled out some coins and fingered through them until he found a half-crown and a florin. "'The rim of the florin,'" Whitbread continued, "'unaccompanied by any other part, will only appear for two moments, just before the whole florin is covered and just after it is uncovered.'" He looked down his spectacles and over the top of the clipping to be sure that Brierly was following him. "'But if the half-crown is allowed to project over the top edge of the florin, while it does not quite reach the bottom edge,'" he read, "'some part of the rim of the florin can be made to persist at the bottom for quite an appreciable time.'" Now Hugh Whitbread looked up from the clipping and, satisfied that Brierly was suitably impressed, continued. "'It will be noted that the florin is never totally eclipsed....'"

"I've heard," Prickett Ellis said to Sasha Richardson (yet another friend of her ambassador father's), "that the experts advise one to choose an open space with a fairly distant easterly horizon."

Whereas a large circle of people had gathered around the handsome and charismatic Ralph Johnson, who was saying he had read that the staff of the Astronomer Royal had arrived in Giggleswick two weeks hence—"Imagine that"—on June 14, and that they were now in position, at a Giggleswick school, with a forty-five-foot-long camera with a six-millimeter lens.

"A camera made in America no less," Herbert Ainsty added, for he, too, read his morning *Times*.

"Oh, this all sounds terribly military and war-like," cried Lady Lovejoy, who had lost a son in the War and did not—on principle, she said—read the papers, for they were full of nothing but bad news.

But just as Richard Dalloway had begun to think about Robbie, to long for him—if only he could have seen Robbie earlier that day, and to muse on and, yes, admit the fact that Robbie was the *now* of life, the present (and the future? he wondered), Lady Bruton snared him, took him off into a corner and immediately began discussing *not* the subject of the moment—the eclipse—nor her host's thirtieth wedding anniversary, but her uncle, the General Sir Talbot Moore, and Richard's biography of her family. She said, with a mortal urgency, that she had something new to tell him.

"Some papers were delivered to me recently," she went on

breathlessly, "from the estate of a deceased cousin; an estate which has long been tied up in legalities." Her voice was low and conspiratorial. "Frankly, I'd forgotten all about it," she said, crossing her arms over her chest. "But I do think that I've uncovered one piece of news which will be of *great* interest to you." She looked around and thought that she best keep this short, get right to the point. "And it is this" (now she was whispering): "It is that my uncle, General Sir Talbot Moore, took a bullet in the War!"

She watched Richard Dalloway's expression as she said the word—"bullet," and she thought that, indeed, he did look surprised. The General had tried to keep it a secret, Lady Bruton added, saying he had recorded it only in his diary as far as anyone knew, of which these papers she had recently been given contained some of the missing pages. But what's more, she said, he extracted the bullet himself!—writing that he could not, nor would he, let his men see him wounded.

"Imagine the strength of mind that took, never mind the physical resilience," she added, "to do that—to take a wound and then extract the bullet oneself. And all the while not letting on, keeping it a secret—what character!" But such was the stock from which she came, Millicent Bruton thought now, fanning her familial tail feathers and stepping back from the corner into which she had pressed Richard Dalloway with the strength of her personality.

Poor Dick, Clarissa thought, looking about the car so as to observe the progress of the party and noticing that Lady Bruton had seemingly backed him into a corner. Though she knew he liked and admired Millicent Bruton—he was writing the biography of her family after all—she thought her husband looked uncomfortable and that he might be in need of rescue. For this was a party, Clarissa reasoned, a party for which he was the host; and Lady Bruton could not talk business to him all night; she could not monopolise him. It was unfair.

"Chagall is in the air," Elizabeth Dalloway thought she overheard someone say. Chagall!—*that* was the name of the painter whose work she'd seen in Paris, that her dream resembled, the painter of cows flying over moons.

Now she leaned her head out the window of the car, remembering the *other* long train ride she had taken that very same morning—in the opposite direction. Oh, she was tired. But just a little air would help wake her up; keep her awake, she thought, licking a finger and then running it along the rims of both of her eyes. And then she saw herself with her head out the window, her hair flying, and she was reminded of Grizzle and how whenever they took him in the motor car, which was more often than not when they were on their way to Fellstree for a weekend, or for the summer, how Grizzle would stick his head out the window, and how his fur would then stand on end and his little pink tongue flap in the wind. What was her poor Grizzle doing that very moment? she wondered—at home alone. Probably sleeping, she thought; dreaming animal dreams.

"What time is it, darling?" Clarissa Dalloway asked Richard, excusing herself to Lady Bruton. And as she did so, Clarissa also sent her husband a signal with her eyes, one only he could have read which said, *Am I right to interrupt? Do you need me?*

And Richard Dalloway stepped out of the corner a bit, in the direction of his wife, looked at his watch and said, "Almost three," and then returned that private look of hers, that signal, with an expression of his own which said, *Yes, thank you darling; save me.*

How she hated such interruptions, Lady Bruton thought, trying to maintain her composure, particularly from the likes of a personage as frivolous and inconsequential as Clarissa Dalloway.

And so Clarissa wrapped her arm about her husband's as she took his hand (for he was hers) and asked Lady Bruton if she was enjoying the party. And Lady Bruton (secretly miffed) said that indeed she was, that *Richard's* idea for the party had been positively grand. "Typically so," she said she might add. And Richard smiled and thanked her, and then, excusing himself, pointed down the car and said that he had to talk to ... (but here his voice trailed off).

So, as in the best choreography, Clarissa stepped in and said how glad she was that Lady Bruton was enjoying the party, for look, there!—the Brunners obviously were not: they had fallen asleep (she laughed).

And there they were—the Brunners, sitting alone together, their faces blank, primeval, as if they were submerged in some other world or some other time; and all the while their heads bounced about as the train continued on its path to North Yorkshire.

(Life is much too short to fall asleep at parties, Clarissa mused.)

Having escaped Millicent Bruton's fierce grasp, Richard Dalloway now sought out John Rosseter, while, at the other end of the car, Mrs. Walker stood at an open window smoking. And noticing the slightly odd (she thought) fellow to her left, dressed all in white but with a green carnation which looked much the worse for wear, she turned to him and asked if he were Irish and if *that* was what the green carnation was for? And he replied that yes, actually, he *was* Irish, or rather that he was descended from the Irish—his paternal grandfather had been born in Dublin. "Black Irish," he added. And then Mrs. Walker, offering him a cigarette (which he declined), said that she had not seen him before, at which point he stuck out his hand and said, "Frank Faber," which Mrs. Walker found odd indeed—that one of her master's guests should introduce himself and offer his hand *to her,* a mere servant. He must be from out in the country somewhere, she thought with a laugh.

"And your youngest, what was his name; how old is he?" Richard Dalloway asked John Rosseter, now that the proud father was boasting about his sons, all but the youngest, that was (for Richard was certain there were five).

"That's Rupert," Rosseter said cagily, looking down. "He's seventeen."

Rupert Rosseter, Richard thought, asking what this Rupert was like, sensing a reluctance on Rosseter's part which he couldn't help but want to push against.

"Oh, he's still in school, you know," John Rosseter said, looking about the car; looking—most likely, Richard thought, for Sally to come to his rescue (but why?). "He's young still; unformed."

And Richard responded that the boy *must* have some interests, for when he was that age....

At which point Rosseter seemingly lost himself, whispered in a full-blown hiss, "He's a Mama's boy, all right? He's Sally's."

Richard Dalloway looked away from John Rosseter now, feeling sorry that he had pushed; sorry, too, for this Rupert—who brought Robbie to mind, for whom he now felt sorry as well, and for whom he longed. So he apologised, but John Rosseter merely shook his head and waved him away, saying that he needn't be sorry, but that he must go and find Sally.

But it seemed to Robbie that Richard had been talking to that same toweringly handsome man all night long, for every time he had looked down the car and seen Richard, which he had just done, there he was, standing right next to and addressing that great, sheltering oak.

He's forgotten me, Robbie thought now, after two more glasses of wine, still in the dark as to where they were all heading (towards their death?). I am but a mere bush, he went on, some delicate, Oriental thing—a Japanese maple, perhaps, compared to that sturdy (if leafless) oak. But what was he to do? He was not a sturdy oak nor could he ever be. Perhaps I should transplant myself, he thought, continuing the botanical metaphor; remove myself to some other garden; to better soil. And then he noticed, standing not two feet away from him, quite the handsome specimen, he thought, one who might even be a fellow traveller, for he looked something like a younger version of Richard. Robbie immediately stood up and introduced himself (thinking *pseudonym be damned),* "Robert Davies," to which the young man responded "Ralph Johnson."

Clarissa now stood with Katherine Truelock and her Eleanor. "Finally!" Katherine said, embracing Clarissa—as the three of them looked over at poor Elizabeth, who had curled up on one of the seats and fallen asleep. "I've been trying to get to you all night," Katherine said.

"And I, you," Clarissa responded.

And so the two old friends began catching up, for they hadn't seen one another in—had it really been three years? Clarissa exclaimed. And then on and on about how the time had flown by, and Clarissa politely trying to include Eleanor in the conversation (though she'd rather not, as Eleanor had always been entirely too hard for her taste), and Katherine saying that their place in Sussex really was not so far from London by train, and that Clarissa had no excuse and that she and Elizabeth must visit that very summer; and just look at how Elizabeth had changed in those three years. "She's a handsome young woman now," Katherine said. "And studying to be a veterinarian no less—Clarissa, you hadn't told us. I'm so proud of her."

Yes, Clarissa said, Elizabeth had blossomed, hadn't she?; she had turned out well. And veterinary school was what she had said she wanted—wanted with all her heart, for she dearly loved animals; so she and Dick had discussed it, and though they knew it would be a long and arduous tenure, they also knew that it would be an experience which would most likely help Elizabeth mature (which, Clarissa said, Elizabeth did need, didn't Katherine think?); and so they had agreed to let her pursue her dream, and in Liverpool no less, for Dick had taken, she said, what he called "the long view," realising that they would have been unable to live with themselves had they knowingly stood in her way, as Dick's father (he had pointed out) had stood in his way—for all Dick had wanted (she said) was to run a farm, but his father had pushed him into law.

Katherine grabbed Clarissa by the upper arms and pulled her close, in an embrace, and said that she was proud of *her* as well.

Clarissa beamed, but she teared up too, thinking of herself and Katherine in such an embrace as young girls—forty, even forty-five years ago—how they had known each other's parents (Katherine had even known Sylvia and was one of the few people still living who had), and just how much life had changed since then (such as, for example, how seldom she and Katherine saw one another now). "Oh, Kathy!" Clarissa cried, now openly embracing her beloved, childhood friend.

And while Mary and Flora were off collecting the loose

glasses and china and silver and napkins strewn here and there about the two cars so that they might begin packing up the baskets, Lucy whispered to Sophie that Wilkins had fallen asleep; "standing up no less," she added, "over there, in that corner" (she pointed and laughed).

And just a couple of seats behind where Wilkins was standing, Sophie whispered: "Look!"

"It's Miss Richardson!" Lucy exclaimed, observing the beautiful young woman as she was kissing a man Lucy did not know, his mackintosh thrown over the both of them.

She was shocked, Lucy said, and Sophie said she thought that Lucy was just jealous.

No, it was not that, Lucy said, it was, well—hadn't Miss Richardson come to the party alone, she whispered, which was shocking indeed, was it not? "Besides, I've *got* a fellow," she added, swooning—"my Paul. Do *you* have someone special?" she asked Sophie, still whispering, and the tall woman seemingly swooped her head down to Lucy's level and nodded sheepishly.

"So *you* live in Bloomsbury, too," handsome Ralph Johnson exclaimed, upon learning that Robert Davies owned a home in Fitzroy Square. "Isn't that a coincidence."

My, but this Johnson is a blockhead, Robbie had decided.

And then (fortunately for him, Robbie mused) the train

began to slow down, accompanied by the familiar hissing sounds and the rhythmic clack, clack, clack of the wheels on the track.

Richard Dalloway looked at his watch. It was 3.30. "We are at Richmond!" he announced. "This is where we get off."

And so people began to stir. Those who had been sleeping sat up straight and looked about; wiped their eyes; smoothed their hair; looked out the window; stood up; yawned. While the others, those who had stayed awake throughout, merely stretched themselves—their arms and legs, readying their bodies for movement after a long dormancy.

We have arrived, Robbie thought, which to him meant that not only would that long, dark, fast tunnelling to nowhere come to an end, but more importantly, he would finally be able to get to Richard.

Slowly, the train groaned to a halt and the crowd began to disembark—Sally and John Rosseter, Sasha Richardson, Hugh Whitbread, and Mina Doyle, so Clarissa Dalloway—who had been one of the first off the train—observed her guests.

"These poor old knees," Mrs. Walker said as she climbed down. "They haven't been the same since those cold nights during the War."

And Lady Vallance almost tripped and fell getting off the train (the lace of her dress somehow caught in the heel of her shoe), her silver-headed walking-stick sent skittering across the ground; but Professor Brierly, of all people, had caught her in his arms.

Whereas Richard Dalloway, upon disembarking, immediately looked up at the sky, which was fleecy and mottled; but (he noted), at least it was not raining. "Look at the long line of omnibuses and motor cars," Hugh Whitbread exclaimed upon seeing what appeared to be an endless caravan of vehicles. "All burning pale yellow lights."

"We have further still to go," Richard announced, at which point there was a moan (it was Mrs. Brunner), now calling for everyone to board the first two omnibuses as soon as possible and saying that—once again—the party would have to be split up.

And so the weary among the travellers piled onto yet another vehicle for yet another journey (such was their attitude), and, once aboard, flung themselves into their seats and glared out the window; though there remained many a gallant one (Lady Bruton, Sasha Richardson, the Rosseters, and Hugh Whitbread among them), who remained upright, awake, alert, and filled with expectation.

But it was now that some of the previous good humour about the nature of the party began to wear off. Mr. and Mrs. Brunner were both openly groaning and complaining; but Sasha

Richardson, who happened to find herself next to them, would have none of it. Where were their manners? Where was their spirit, their sense of adventure? Their souls are dead, she thought; life is too short to listen to the likes of them. She walked away.

And when the omnibuses finally began to move, to ramble, Robert Davies, having once again managed to board a vehicle separate from Richard Dalloway, began to wonder why he had bothered, why he had troubled to come at all, for where had it got him? Richmond, that was where.

But Richard wanted to talk to Clarissa, *needed* to talk with her, he said, for he was afraid that he had accidentally offended John Rosseter. And so he asked her to sit with him and, once seated, began to tell her the story (whispering it in her ear) of what had happened.

And Clarissa could see, as she listened to her husband's whisperings, she could see that a few of their guests—those who were looking—thought that she and Richard were engaging in some sort of intimacy (the phrase *whispering sweet nothings* came to her), some sort of intimacy appropriate to the occasion of their thirtieth wedding anniversary, which (she thought) was all for the best, for otherwise it might have appeared rude.

No, she did not think he had done anything wrong, she answered him, it was obviously a subject which for John

Rosseter must be terribly sensitive. But don't worry, darling, she said; there they were, Sally and John, sitting towards the front (she gestured towards them with her head). She would go and talk to them, not—of course—mentioning anything about *this*; she would go and talk to them and—in five or ten minutes—he should come and join them. It would be all right, she patted his hand.

"Look!" Lady Hosford exclaimed to Elizabeth, staring out the window (for the sun was rising), and the two had somehow ended up sitting together. "Just look at how the fields seem to be ablaze with June grasses."

"I've never seen so many sheep," Elizabeth answered her, equally excited, for this was a part of the country she had never before visited, and she loved its wildness. "Do you know the name of those red tasselled plants?" she asked Lady Hosford, who responded that she did not, but that indeed they *were* lovely, weren't they?

"Just look at all these adorable little Yorkshire farms," Lady Vallance said to Professor Brierly as she patted the hand she had held ever since he had saved her life (or such was her version of what had transpired). "So many of them still lit up— at this hour. Oh, and look! Look at that family, there (she pointed), standing out and waving to us" (she waved back).

But all Professor Brierly could think of was Dantë's *Inferno*, for surely there could be nothing more hellish than this—finding oneself suddenly in the clutches of a very grateful old lady merely because one had—out of sheer humanity—prevented her from falling (which she had misconstrued as saving her life). But if she continued to go on and on like this, he thought, I should like to *take* her life.

Hugh Whitbread, sitting alone and studying the landscape (for he must remember *everything* so as to tell Evelyn), now pulled out the compass he had brought along for just such purposes as this, for he wanted to know in what direction they were headed. He consulted the compass—the arrow was between the North and the West. *Northwest*, he thought, momentarily confused. North he could certainly understand, but West? Did that make sense? He knew that the North Sea would be to his right, which was East, and he would have thought they would be heading in *that* direction. But perhaps (he thought now), perhaps there is some higher point inland which gives a better eastern view. Yes, he thought, pleased with himself for his common sense in figuring it out, that *must* be it.

Sitting two seats behind Hugh Whitbread was Sally Rosseter, who was feeling somewhat put out with her husband (she told him), because after all it was *her Rupert* that he and

Richard had been discussing. Nevertheless, she said, he should think nothing of it; for Richard Dalloway was a bumbling, ineffectual...Clarissa, darling (Sally exclaimed, as Clarissa Dalloway sat down behind them).

No, Lady Hosford said, she did not know the name of that vast castle they were passing on the right at that very moment, did anyone else? (No, no one else seemed to know it either.) But yes, it *was* splendid, Lady Hosford said; but then she turned back to Elizabeth and said (with a dismissive wave of the hand) that she had seen her share of castles; but they had been discussing George Eliot's *Middlemarch*.

Elizabeth could not believe the pleasant time she was having with Lady Hosford, after having known her for all those years (all of her life, really) and *never* having liked her. But here they were, discussing *Middlemarch*, and now Lady Hosford was agreeing with her that Dorothea never should have married in the first place.

"But do you think it a flaw in the novel?" she asked Lady Hosford. And Lady Hosford, pleased that her opinion mattered to Elizabeth and that she was being paid this respect and attention, brushed at Elizabeth's long hair with her hand and said that yes, she was afraid that it *was* a flaw in the novel, a mis-step on the part of George Eliot; then told Elizabeth that she could still recall her excitement when, from week to week, *Middlemarch* was coming out in *Harper's Weekly*. "We were living in America at the time—father was teaching at Harvard College"; she said she must have been—what?—about seventeen or eighteen.

But just where in China was their son, Clarissa asked Sally and John Rosseter, still trying to thaw them out after several minutes of conversation; she knew that getting them to talk about their *other* sons would do the trick.

"That's Gordon, isn't it?" she went on. "The one in China?"

"Yes," Rosseter himself turned around to answer her, "Gordon is in Peking."

"Oh, that must be terribly exciting for him," Clarissa said. At which point Richard Dalloway joined his wife on the seat behind the Rosseters and, observing John looking out the window, put a hand on his shoulder and said "Fascinating country, no?" But before waiting for a response he went on to say that though he would not want to live there, for it would be much too harsh, he *did* think that it *would* be a splendid place to pass a week's or a month's holiday, in the proper season of course—hunting, fishing, sailing the lakes, walking....

"Indeed it would," John Rosseter exclaimed. "You know," he added, smiling at Richard Dalloway and hoping to indicate (without having to say it) that all was forgiven, "it is not unlike Shropshire in ways."

And all the while Robert Davies sat alone in the last seat of the omnibus, his body absorbing the jerks and shocks of the bumpy ride—bouncing here, jerking there, like a marionette.

"Just look at those two farm women hanging out of the upper windows," Lady Vallance pointed. "And in their nightclothes, no less. But one must admit that it is a charming sight, wouldn't you agree, Professor?"

At which point Professor Brierly got up, excused himself, and made his way towards the back of the bus, offering no explanation whatsoever, for he had had enough!

My, but she hoped the poor dear hadn't suddenly taken ill, Lady Vallance thought, what with the thin air at such a high altitude; and he did seem somewhat delicate.

And indeed, the omnibuses were now climbing immensely steep hills and at such an incline that the passengers had to strain to stay aright. And as the omnibuses made their way, ever so slowly, they were overtaken and then passed by the occasional motor car shooting ahead.

"An accident would be perfectly natural," a nervous Hugh Whitbread announced to Mira Cartwright, whose hat had just been knocked off her head when the omnibus shifted and jerked and began to take yet another steep hill. "An accident should not be unexpected in a situation like this."

But hearing what Hugh had just said, Richard, Clarissa, Sally, and John exchanged looks, and then John Rosseter burst out laughing, followed by Sally and Clarissa. "Same old Hugh," Sally said, remembering how she had once told him, amidst an argument about women's rights, that he represented everything that was most detestable about middle-class life. It was true. And then Hugh had kissed her, on the lips in the smoking-room, to punish her—he said—for saying that women should have the vote.

Richard, however, feeling responsible for the well-being of his passengers, the party-goers—his guests, jokingly said that he wanted to shake Hugh. For it was so typical of him, Richard thought; he is so like an old maid. Old Hugh Whitbread, poor soul—for he had been old at twenty.

But beyond Hugh Whitbread, Richard now spotted Mrs. Walker and that servant of Lady Hosford's, Miss What's-hername?, sitting in adjacent seats and smoking cigarettes, their faces red with laughter. It served to remind him that he never had done anything about that situation; but it seemed to have righted itself (he thought, rather amused).

And now the omnibuses slowed down as they arrived at what the driver announced was "the highest point—Bardon Fell."

What now? Robbie asked himself as the omnibus came to a full stop. Now that he was sobering up (for he had been drinking cup after cup of tea), he began to panic: what would he do? What was he doing there? He fingered his father's wedding ring so as to calm himself. It would be all right. He would remain calm. And when the time came, he reasoned, when it seemed prudent (and provident), he would simply walk up to Richard and—and what? Should he embrace him? Or merely shake his hand?

Climbing down off of the bus, Elizabeth Dalloway said that she was astonished at the number of people. Scanning the huge moor, she noticed butts for grouse-shooting and still more sheep scattered here and there; she told Katherine and Eleanor, with whom she'd met up again, and Lady Hosford, who had joined their group, that she had just realised they were in Brontë country.

The four women looked around. All about them people were camping beside their cars; and there (Eleanor pointed), there were so many tracks in the grass where, up ahead, at the edge of the highest point (their eyes followed the tracks), so many had already taken up their positions.

But all Lady Bruton, who had stepped off the bus behind them, could think of, looking about, was how—in battle, strategically establishing one's troops on this Bardon Fell would give one a great vantage point. But then she immediately realised the danger of it too, for an entire infantry could just as well be trapped there; trapped and ambushed!

The air was thin, Richard Dalloway noticed, thin but fresh and cool too, as he called everyone together to walk to the highest point overlooking Richmond. And as they began walking, Richard noticed that off to their left a group of vendors had set up tables selling tinted glass, film, and protective lenses (among other things), which the experts advised one must use when viewing the eclipse. He had read about it in the *Times*; such protection, it was said, was absolutely necessary, and so he would buy them for everyone. He would need fifty-eight, he told the vendor.

"It's a regular circus," Hugh Whitbread cried.

"But look at the sun," John Rosseter said (pointing), it was at that point a mere gold spot covered over by a soft grey cloud.

But someone not of the party answered that it was early yet and they would just have to wait.

And now the crowd, passing out the protectors, looked out at the horizon and over the valley that was Richmond, which sparkled with a few lights here and there.

People were stamping to keep warm, or huddling close together, some standing outside tents, others beside the feeding sheep; while others, like the Brunners, had bought horse blankets, which were also being sold by some of the more enterprising vendors.

And Katherine Truelock, standing with her Eleanor, announced to the crowd that she had just met someone, an admirable old woman with a wireless, who told her that the BBC had announced that they were sending broadcast signals (which they had started at 4.30), and that during the critical period from 6.22 to 6.26, single seconds would be sent out.

"Imagine that!" Hugh Whitbread exclaimed, looking at his watch—it was 5.15. "Broadcast signals every second for four minutes; why that's two-hundred forty signals!" It was unprecedented, he said, unprecedented in the history of the BBC so far as he knew.

"So he can do his numbers," Professor Brierly said wryly, once again approaching Frank Faber.

"It is unquestionably *Jane Eyre*," Lady Hosford said, responding to Katherine Truelock's claim that *Villette* was Charlotte Brontë's masterpiece (while adding, with a laugh, that Eleanor preferred *Shirley*).

But Elizabeth said that she too, like Lady Hosford, was partial to *Jane Eyre,* because she honestly believed it was responsible for her going to veterinary school. *Jane Eyre.* And Miss Kilman, who was my history tutor." (There! Elizabeth thought;

I have said it. At last I have introduced Miss Kilman, and she is among us.)

"Did you say Kilman?" Eleanor asked. "That wouldn't be Doris Kilman, would it?"

"You know her!" Elizabeth cried, and Katherine looked puzzled.

"Why, yes—you remember her, Kate, at suffragette meetings; we were so impressed with her dedication."

But Katherine responded that no, she couldn't honestly say that she did remember a Doris Kilman.

But Elizabeth was satisfied; someone beside herself had known and remembered Miss Kilman.

"And we are here upon a darkling plain..." Professor Brierly said, to no one in particular.

But it was more difficult, Robbie thought, moving about so as to avoid Brierly, more difficult now that they were no longer in the contained areas of train car and omnibus, but were instead individually moving about such a vast moor. Where, for example, was Richard? He had not seen him since they'd disembarked. And it seemed possible that he *would not* see Richard again as long as they remained here; or conversely, that he might bump into Richard *or Mrs. Dalloway* at any moment (for he had finally seen her identified; a handsome, white-haired, middle-aged woman). It was dangerous; but what should he do? Remaining in one place would most likely serve him best, he resolved; remaining in one place and staying alert. Perhaps he would see Richard's daughter, Elizabeth, and he could ask her if she had seen her father.

Now looking about the moor he noticed a tall, thin woman standing with another, shorter, rather masculine-looking woman, not more than ten feet away. Isn't that Virginia Woolf? he asked himself. He had been introduced to her once at a party in London for one of Faber's authors. He saw her only in profile (now she turned towards him); yes, he believed it was—Mrs. Woolf—and her friend Vita Sackville-West.

"There's Virginia!" Lady Vallance cried, interrupting Clarissa Dalloway as she spotted a tall, elegant figure standing in the grass talking with another woman. "Why, I haven't seen her in ages."

"Who?" Clarissa Dalloway asked.

"Virginia Woolf," Lady Vallance said. "And that's that Sackville-West woman with her." And then Lady Vallance whispered something inaudible into Clarissa Dalloway's ear.

"Where?" Clarissa asked, looking about.

"There," Lady Vallance pointed. "I overheard someone in the crowd say that they had seen her get on the train, but I didn't think much of it."

"She's beautiful," Clarissa said, "much more so than her pictures reflect. Do you know her?"

"Oh my, yes; I've known her since she was a child; my parents knew her parents, you see, when we lived in Hyde Park—what? some forty years ago now. We have the same birthday, you know," Lady Vallance added, "twenty-five January; though I am twenty-six years older." The older woman continued to look over at the younger, now-famous author as if she were looking at her own past. "Little Virginia Stephen," she said wistfully. "Such a gloomy household, the Stephens," she added. "Mother and Father didn't approve of them." She seemed lost in her own reverie. "Little Virginia always had the biggest eyes; they were like saucers." Now she looked away. "But I haven't seen much of her over the years."

And Clarissa Dalloway said that she should like to meet Mrs. Woolf; would Lady Vallance introduce her?

But just as Lady Vallance had said that of course she would introduce them and she and Clarissa had turned to walk over to the two writers, the Mrs. Woolf and Sackville-West were joined by two men ("probably their husbands," Lady Vallance speculated) and then walked away as a foursome, disappearing into the expectant crowd.

"Richard, I have just heard," Lady Bruton announced to Mr.

Dalloway in her best, booming voice, "I have just heard that for this event some Parisian has chartered flights by the Imperial Airways from Paris to Croydon at ten guineas a seat. Ten guineas!" Now wasn't that just like the French? she asked him.

But his attention was distracted by the servants—Wilkins, Lucy, Mrs. Walker, the three specially hired girls, and Lady Hosford's Miss What'shername, all of whom seemed to be having a riotous good time together. I am tired of Millicent Bruton's prejudices (he thought), and thinking, too, of his biography, he hoped that such irrationally held views did not pervade the entire family.

He excused himself and moved nearer to where the servants were sitting. They were teasing Wilkins, particularly Mrs. Walker, as she smoked: "But do ye have a lady-friend, Mr. Wilkins?" she asked, amidst giggling from the others. "Or maybe you prefer the boys?" she went on, at which Sophie whooped with laughter, flapping her white apron.

Richard Dalloway felt himself colouring and moved on, away from where the members of the party had gathered. He needed a moment; it had been a long trip. And reviewing the events of yesterday and last evening, perhaps inevitably, he thought now, he found himself thinking of Robbie. He actually thought he had seen Robbie's face earlier, briefly, amidst the crowd on Bardon Fell, but just as immediately he dismissed the idea, recognising wishful thinking when he saw it. It was absurd—he had clearly seen someone who had reminded him of Robbie; or he had imagined Robbie.

I love Clarissa, he thought to himself now, standing alone, away from the crowd, hands shoved deep into the pockets of his trousers, staring at the ground. But I love Robbie, too; I must admit that once and for all. I love Robbie; I miss him; and I want him: my life is incomplete without him.

But then he noticed Sasha Richardson, whom he'd known since she was a baby—the ambassador's daughter; Sasha, who still called him "Mr. Dalloway," also standing alone—in her sleeveless dress, shivering, her arms wrapped around herself.

"You must be freezing, dear," he said, walking over to her.

Sasha nodded, her teeth chattering.

Richard put an arm around the beautiful young woman, saying, "Here, let me warm you." Then he wrapped his jacket about her shoulders.

She smiled, thanked him, and said that she had been standing there trying to imagine what it must be like to be married to someone for thirty years; that she couldn't imagine it for herself. And then she turned suddenly to Richard Dalloway and looked him in the eye, and he could see that she had been crying.

"Are you happy?" she asked.

Richard Dalloway was startled, taken aback even, for one didn't ask such questions in polite society; and yet he understood Sasha's impulse.

"The short answer, dear Sasha, is, yes, I am happy."

Sasha wondered if he was being truthful, or if he was lying, as people usually did about the question of happiness. Nevertheless, she took Richard Dalloway's hand and said, "Please tell me how you and Mrs. Dalloway came to be married."

"Oh, my," Richard said, with Sasha's arm in his as they began to stroll towards the party-goers. "It was so long ago now" (and here he looked off, as if searching for that past on the horizon). "Well, I believe you know that I first met Clarissa at Bourton, her family's summer home. And she was—what?—a vision of loveliness. Much like yourself," he added.

She ignored the compliment. "Were you in love with her immediately?"

"No," he answered. "No, not really; I couldn't be because, you see, there was another chap—perhaps you've heard his name: Peter Walsh? And he and Clarissa were quite involved with each other at the time...."

"How did you win her over then?"

Richard Dalloway was once again stunned by Sasha

Richardson's directness. He laughed; he guessed this was the way of the younger generation. "Well, I don't know, quite; it just—happened; I suppose, in the end, because it was what Clarissa wanted."

A voice in the crowd called out that it was 5.50, and both of them paused to observe the sky. Richard Dalloway pointed out the thin spots in some of the clouds. The question now, he said to Sasha, is whether the sun will show through a cloud when the time comes.

"And then what?" Sasha implored, returning to the subject of his and Mrs. Dalloway's courtship.

"Why so suddenly curious, Sasha?" he smiled.

But she only shrugged, and for a moment a silence hung in the air between them as they continued to walk.

"Well, I know that Clarissa and Peter had some terrible rows when she called it off between them," he went on. "Everyone at Bourton seemed to know," he laughed; "it was rather awful. And Clarissa's best friend at the time, Sally Seton, now Sally Rosseter, did you meet her?" (Sasha nodded.) "Sally didn't much like me and made no attempt to hide the fact, which was difficult." He paused to take a deep breath. "But somehow Clarissa persevered and we began escaping into London together, which, well, you probably can't imagine this, having grown up in the city—much as our Elizabeth takes it for granted—but, for Clarissa and me, who were raised in the country and had rarely set foot in London, it was sheer heaven."

He paused again, not wanting to go on too much, but Sasha merely looked at him imploringly, seemingly fascinated by his narrative.

"We would ride the train in together from Bourton, get off at Waterloo, and then walk across the Hungerford footbridge. And it was as if the city was ours, Sasha; as if it welcomed us." (He wondered if she could understand this.) "Well, so it is when one is in love, I suppose," he added defensively, feeling slightly embarrassed. He went on. "And then we simply walked. All over the city; indeed, just as we were falling in love, so—together—did we fall in love with the city; we got to know it quite well, too."

"And do you walk still?" Sasha asked.

"Oh no," Mr. Dalloway said. "No, we haven't really walked in the city together for years; there hasn't been time."

Sasha stopped and turned to him, for that was what she minded so much, that people should stop walking. "But isn't that sad?" she asked.

He hadn't much thought of it, he said, but he supposed that there *was* something rather sad about it. Again there was a silence between them, but this time it felt awkward, uncomfortable. "We should be getting back," he said, checking his watch.

CLARISSA DALLOWAY STOOD alone in the odd, pre-eclipse light, her search for Richard having taken her there. And as she stood alone her mind took that characteristic downward turn, so that all she could think of, waiting there in the chill, was the end of the world, when time had run out (where she imagined Aunt Helena, Sylvia, and her father and mother were waiting for her). Or was it the beginning, before time? Whichever, she thought now—this was the largest window ever at which she would stand waiting.

But then her reverie was interrupted as she noticed the sun's rays breaking through the bottom of the clouds. She must find Richard (she thought), for she needed him; and she didn't want to experience this without him. Then, suddenly, there he was, standing at her side.

"I've been looking all over for you, dear," she said, grasping his hand.

He told her that he had been talking with poor Sasha Richardson; rather consoling her, he thought.

Clarissa looked at him quizzically, and he continued.

"She told me she couldn't imagine being married for

thirty years and wanted to know all about our courtship—that sort of thing."

"Poor dear," his wife said. "I do worry about her. But I presume you told her *just* how marvelous it was," Clarissa said playfully.

"Indeed I did," he smiled. "For it *was*," he added. He briefly looked down at the ground and then returned his gaze to his wife. "It served to remind me that we haven't much walked in London together for years," he said. "Sasha said she thought that rather sad."

"No, we haven't," she agreed. "I daresay it's been at least fifteen or twenty years."

"But now that I have the time again, we must." He squeezed her hand. "Just as we used to."

"6.20!" a wizened old woman called out through her megaphone. Silence immediately fell over the crowd as—*en masse*—they now stared up at the sky.

The clouds were sweeping, moving along at a great pace; then sailing fast across the sun; then red streamers appeared, now a golden haze.

Someone in the crowd announced that after this it would be over until 1999 (and Richard Dalloway thought to himself that 1999 was a year so far away, so remote-seeming, that he couldn't even imagine it).

Robbie felt spooked, haunted even, by the scene on Bardon

Fell. It was as if they were all druids (he thought, standing alone and looking about); as if the world was—somehow—dead; he felt frightened; he was alone; where was Richard?

Over the gathering crowd now there were great blue spaces in the clouds. Then suddenly, the colour began going out—the clouds were turning pale; and then a reddish black colour prevailed: nothing could be seen through the clouds. Now all colours faded as it became darker and darker, as at the beginning of a violent storm; and people were saying that this must be the shadow, this must be the shadow.

"6.22!"

Now everyone began pulling out the protective lenses Richard Dalloway had bought for them. He handed his wife hers from his shirt pocket.

There he stood with his Clarissa (he thought), hand in hand, viewing the eclipse. It was their thirtieth wedding anniversary and the party he had given for her had been a success. And yet he missed Robbie.

The sheep began bleating, as if they were frightened. And then the sun disappeared. It was like a sudden plunge, Richard Dalloway thought, a sudden plunge when one least expected it. One felt terribly small, minute, and inconsequential—like a blade of grass, an ant, or one of these sheep; and the cold increased.

Suddenly, then, in the darkness, he saw an apparition—there was Robbie, standing at his side. But then the sky, as if it were a rebounding ball, took colour again as the light came back—in the valley, over the hills, at first glittering and aethereal, and then normal. It was impressive. And it was over.

"How bracing!" Lady Hosford exclaimed.

Eleanor Gibson put her arm around Katherine's waist and, without saying anything—for so united were their minds after twenty-four years together—the two women thought, as one, about Caroline Furness, that American woman from the observatory at Vassar College....

"I know what you're thinking," Katherine said, for both of them had been active in the suffragette movement before leaving London, and Caroline Furness's presence, her very inclusion in the scientific community, had indeed made it a proud day for all women.

And though Sasha Richardson stood alone, Richard Dalloway's jacket still wrapped around her shoulders, the eclipse had somehow brought with it a feeling of warmth and well-being she had never known. It was as if she'd had a vision of the future, a surprising certainty that she *would* find someone, just as Mr. Dalloway had found Mrs. Dalloway, and that she would not—contrary to all prior expectations—have to live her life alone.

Claire Milan kissed Robert Haydon full on the lips, thinking that they would remember this moment forever, for they were now engaged.

But for Lady Vallance, the sun's brief disappearance—all she could think of was how it seemed like a trial run of sorts, a simulation of how, in a fairly short time, five years from now, or tomorrow, her own life would soon be eclipsed.

Still holding his wife's hand, Richard Dalloway looked to his right and again saw the figure of Robbie. Only this time he realised, with nothing but pleasure, that it was no mere apparition but Robbie himself, in the flesh, standing at his side.

He looked to Clarissa, who was marvelling over the eclipse with Lady Hosford. (It was all right, he told himself; she understood.) Oblivious to any concern about appearances or to what might or might not be the coincidence of just *how* Robbie happened to be there, all he could think was that this might be his last chance to prove to himself that his soul was not dead.

He tightened his grasp on Clarissa's hand (and, still talking with Lady Hosford, she squeezed his hand in return). Then, there, in the sunlight, amidst the crowd, he took Robbie's hand in his, briefly, without even looking at him, and then he let it go. Only for a moment, but it was enough. It was a beginning.

The Author

Robin Lippincott is the author of *The Real, True Angel,* a collection of short stories published in 1996 by Fleur-de-Lis Press. His fiction and nonfiction have appeared in *The New York Times Book Review, The American Voice, The Literary Review, Provincetown Arts,* and many other magazines; he was awarded fellowships to Yaddo in 1997 and 1998. Born and raised in the South, he has lived in Boston for twenty years. He is currently at work on a novel.

Donna Coveney

ACKNOWLEDGMENTS

Thanks to—Kirkby Tittle and Steve Bauer—readers, writers, and good friends whose enthusiasm and encouragement during the writing of this book was invaluable. And to Martha Corazon, Angelo Monaco, and Lee Salkovitz, who offered their thoughts on aesthetic (and other) matters.

Thanks to—my sisters, Marcia Kay Lippincott and Cindy Brown, and my parents, Robert W. and Marcia L. Lippincott; and to Michael Anderson, Bruce Aufhammer, Ellen Balber, Bonnie Barber, Gaynor Blandford, Joe Caldwell, Michael Carroll, Donna Coveney, Eileen Fitzpatrick, Anne Hoppe, Bob O'Handley, Sheila Ortiz Taylor, Frankie Paino, Rick Reinkraut, Louise Riemer, Frederick Smock, and to my agent, Malaga Baldi, whose love for the book helped see me through.

I am also grateful to the Corporation of Yaddo, which gave me—twice in as many years—the opportunity to work on my next book while this one awaited a publisher.